"Fast paced and well plotted . . . While comparisons will be made with Turow, Grisham and Connelly, Jagger is a new voice on the legal/thriller scene. I recommend you check out this debut book, but be warned . . . you are not going to be able to put it down."
CRIME SPREE MAGAZINE

"A chilling story well told. The pace never slows in this noir thriller, taking readers on a stark trail of fear."
CAROLYN G. HART, N.Y. Times and USA Today Bestselling Author

"Verdict: The pacing is relentless in this debut, a hard-boiled novel with a shocking ending. The supershort chapters will please those who enjoy a James Patterson–style page-turner"
LIBRARY JOURNAL

A "clever and engrossing mystery tale involving gorgeous women, lustful men and scintillating suspense."
FOREWORD MAGAZINE

"Part of what makes this thriller thrilling is that you sense there to be connections among all the various subplots; the anticipation of their coming together keeps the pages turning."
BOOKLIST

"This is one of the best thrillers I've read yet."
New Mystery Reader Magazine

"A superb thriller and an exceptional read."
MIDWEST BOOK REVIEW

"Verdict: This fast-paced book offers fans of commercial thrillers a twisty, action-packed thrill ride."
LIBRARY JOURNAL

"Another masterpiece of action and suspense."
NEW MYSTERY READER MAGAZINE

HONG KONG WOMAN

Thriller Publishing Group, Inc.

HONG KONG WOMAN

R.J. JAGGER
JIM MICHAEL HANSEN

Thriller Publishing Group, Inc.

HONG KONG WOMAN

Thriller Publishing Group, Inc.

Copyright©2009RJJagger

Library of Congress Control Number: Available

ISBN 978-1-937888-70-1

For Eileen

Acknowledgements

Thanks to the many wonderful readers, booksellers, editors, publishers, agents, audio producers, book reviewers, authors, groups (including International Thriller Writers and Mystery Writers of America), proofreaders and other kind-hearted souls who amplified my efforts and who encouraged me with positive vibes over the years. Without you this book would have never happened.

DAY ONE

August 3
Monday

1

August 3
Monday Night

Nick Teffinger, the head of Denver's homicide unit, drove home through a dark night in the middle of a nasty thunderstorm. The wipers swung at full speed and still couldn't keep up with the slop. Duran Duran's "Rio" came from the radio, loud, the way it was supposed to be. Teffinger sang when the chorus came up, barely able to hear his own 34-year-old voice. Ten minutes later when he turned into his driveway, something strange happened.

The headlights swept across a person sitting on the front steps, in the weather.

He stopped the vehicle in front of the garage, killed the engine, studied the figure for a heartbeat and then swung his six-foot-two frame out. The storm assaulted him immediately, almost horizontal, squeezing into his eyes and sucking at his breath.

The person turned out to be a woman, an Asian

woman, very attractive even in her battered state.

She stood up and shouted over the weather, "Are you Nick Teffinger?" The words were in English with a foreign accent.

"I am."

"I need to talk to you."

He saw no car on the street.

She had no purse in her hands.

"Come on in."

Inside, he got a better look at her. She was hypnotically beautiful, about twenty-eight, five-five, in nice shape, with green eyes and thick raven hair halfway down her back. She wore jeans and a black T-shirt, both of which dripped like waterfalls onto the tile.

"We need to get you dried off," Teffinger said.

She cocked her head.

"Don't you want to know who I am first?"

"Sure, who are you?"

"My name's d'Asia," she said. "I'm from Hong Kong."

"D'Asia?"

"Right."

"You're a long way from home, d'Asia from Hong Kong."

"Trust me, I've noticed."

Teffinger gave her a long-sleeve shirt from his closet, pointed her to the bathroom and said, "I'll be in the garage when you're done. Whatever you do, don't look under my mattress." He was sitting in the dark behind the wheel of the '67 Corvette, drinking a Bud Light and watching the storm through the windshield, when she showed up. Her hair was still wet but now combed.

She got in the passenger seat.

He handed her a glass of cold white wine.

"This is my favorite thing in the world," he said, "watching a storm from right here."

Lightning arced across the sky as if to prove it.

D'Asia took a swallow of wine and studied him.

"So how long were you sitting out there in the rain waiting for me?" Teffinger asked.

She shrugged.

"I don't know, half an hour maybe."

"I'm impressed," Teffinger said. "I've had people wait for me that long before, but they were always someone I owed money to. I don't owe you money, do I?"

She chuckled.

"No."

"Good, because I don't have any," he said. "You're sitting in all my money."

She smiled.

"So who are you d'Asia and what's going on?"

She sighed.

"Too much," she said. "Are you sure you want to know?"

She told him about how she was a model from Hong Kong. Someone had been following her for the last week or so. She didn't know who or why but was absolutely convinced that she had been targeted for a hit and that the execution date was here. She had a feeling that the source was someone wealthy and influential and powerful, but couldn't point to any specific, concrete facts to support it.

The tension got to be too much.

She had to get out of the country.

She flew to the states, to Denver to be precise, to see Teffinger to be even more precise.

"I don't get it," Teffinger said. "Why me? What do I have to do with any of this?"

"Nothing, really," she said. "It's just that Billy Shek said you'd help me, if I asked."

Billy Shek?

"I never heard of him," Teffinger said. "Who's Billy Shek?"

"You don't know him?"

"No."

"He's a photographer."

"From Hong Kong?"

"Right."

"I don't know any photographers from any-where," Teffinger said. "Much less Hong Kong."

"Well he knows you," she said, "or maybe he just knows of you. I'm not real clear on it, now that you say you don't know him."

Teffinger racked his brain.

Billy Shek.

Hong Kong.

Still nothing.

"Does he go by any other name?"

She shrugged and didn't know.

Teffinger drained the rest of his beer and cracked open another one. "So what is it that you want from me, exactly?" he asked.

"I want you to help me."

"Help you how?"

"I don't know," she said. "All I know is that I don't want to die."

Silence.

"Well, you did fly halfway around the world and then sat out in a storm," he said. "I guess that entitles you to something."

She studied him.

"Does that mean you'll help?"

He nodded.

"Yeah, I guess it does." He saw doubt in her eyes and added, "I'm serious."

"Really?"

"Yeah. You have my promise."

She exhaled.

Then she said, "I didn't expect you to look like this."

"Like what?"

She didn't answer.

Instead she leaned over and brought her mouth to his, dangerously close. The warmth of her breath filled his senses. Then she kissed him. He immediately knew his life had just changed. How far and how big, he couldn't tell, but a change had most definitely come.

2

August 3
Monday Night

Teffinger knew he shouldn't allow himself to get attracted to this mysterious woman. She was from Hong Kong. He wasn't. There was a whole lot of blue watery earth between them. But he was already lost in her hair, her eyes, her song-like voice, her slightly crooked smile and the way she walked. He could already picture having her around for a long, long time and never looking back.

One thing did bother him, though.

She was insistent that she had no idea who was targeting her, or why.

That, in Teffinger's experience, was unlikely.

You don't work yourself into a position like that without having at least some inkling of where everything suddenly went batshit crazy. Still, he had to admit, while unlikely, it wasn't necessarily impossible. Maybe she had seen something that she shouldn't have and never even realized it. Maybe she simply got herself on the radar screen of some random sociopath.

She did come halfway around the world to get shelter. You don't do that unless you're actually scared. So, if she was that scared, why wouldn't she tell him what was going on? He'd be able to protect her better if she did.

There were lots of questions that needed answers.

Right now, however, she was suddenly leading him by the hand into the bedroom as the weather outside raged against the windows and the roof and the sides of the house.

Ordinarily he'd be all for it, but he stopped at the door.

She was vulnerable.

She was in fear.

She might be doing what she was planning on doing as a means of payment. He'd done some low things in his life but he'd never taken advantage of a woman at risk and wasn't about to now.

"You don't have to do this," he said. "I'm not looking for anything."

She chuckled.

"You think this is for you?"

Lightning exploded.

He said, "I'll be on the couch. Get some sleep."

"Are you sure?"

"Yes."

"Can you at least sleep in the bed with me? I want to feel safe. It's been so long."

"You'll be safe," Teffinger said. "Don't worry."

Then he closed the door and headed for the couch.

Sometime later, which could have been ten minutes or three hours, a strange noise wrestled him out of a deep sleep. He kept his eyes closed but let himself wake up just enough to focus. The storm hammered the house and rattled the windows.

Above that, he heard nothing.

He listened harder.

He still got nothing.

Then a strange crashing vibration came from the bedroom. He bounded in and flicked on the lights. What he saw he could hardly believe. D'Asia was on the floor, on her back. A woman with blond hair was on top of her, trying to force a knife into her face. Teffinger took two steps towards the attacker and then lunged through the air.

Instead of reaching her, he fell short.

His forehead caught the edge of the bed and exploded with pain.

His body crashed to the floor and landed on his shoulder.

"Nick!"

He muscled up, desperate, and managed to swing an arm at the attacker before everything went black.

His first thought when he came to was that no one had killed him while he was passed out. The lights were off and the room was dark. A motionless body was on the carpet next to him.

He shook it.

No response came.

"D'Asia!"

She didn't move.

It was then that he saw a knife sticking out of the woman's chest. He pulled it out and threw it across the room.

No.

No!

No!

No!

He laid his head on her leg.

Then the lights suddenly turned on.

He looked over and saw d'Asia.

Then he looked at the body. It was an Asian woman, a second Asian woman, with a blond wig, someone he had never seen before.

"Who is she?" he asked.

"I don't know."

"You don't have any idea?"

"No," d'Asia said. "I've never seen her before in my life."

"Was she the one following you?"

"I don't know. Probably."

The dead woman was about thirty and athletic. Teffinger went through her pockets and found both U.S. and Hong Kong currency, but no wallet or car keys or anything else.

"No I.D.," he said.

D'Asia looked distant and said, "I just killed

someone."

Teffinger grunted.

"It was self-defense."

"I don't want to go to jail."

"You won't go to jail," Teffinger said. "It was you or her. There's nothing to worry about. I'm a witness to the whole thing."

The knife was a high-quality weapon with a 6-inch serrated blade and a black composite handle inscribed with red Asian characters.

"We need to make a report," Teffinger said.

"To who?"

"The Lakewood P.D.," Teffinger said.

"But you're with Denver, right?"

He nodded.

"Right."

"So you won't be the one investigating?"

"No. I couldn't anyway. I'm a witness."

D'Asia stood up.

Her shirt had blood on it.

"I don't trust anyone else," she said. "I only trust you."

"Then trust me, there's nothing to worry about."

She said nothing.

Instead she stepped into the bathroom and closed the door. When she came out, she had her jeans and T-shirt on. Both were still wet but no longer dripping.

"What are you doing?" Teffinger asked.

She kissed him, hard and passionately, then ran down the hall and shouted over her shoulder, "I can't outrun this. I need to go back to Hong Kong and meet it head on."

Before he could stop her, she was out the front door running down the street, disappearing into the storm.

"D'Asia, come back here!"

She didn't come back—not in five minutes, not in ten, not in thirty. Teffinger reached for the phone six different times to call the Lakewood P.D. but never dialed. He took a shower, grabbed a Bud Light and watched the storm from behind the wheel of the '67.

An hour passed.

He drank three more beers.

D'Asia didn't return. She wouldn't.

He knew that now.

Then he realized why he hadn't reported the incident. It was because he was coming up with a plan. When he realized what it was, it shocked him.

It was dangerous. It was wrong.

It could end his career, but deep down he had no choice.

DAY TWO

August 4
Tuesday

3

August 4
Tuesday Morning

Prarie Dubois dragged her 22-year-old French body out of bed and pulled the curtain back to see what the Parisian morning looked like. The first rays of daylight were just starting to wash the City of Light with a golden patina. A barge moved slowly up the Seine. The sky had a few rough clouds, but not many. She threw on sweatpants and a T-shirt, pulled long blond hair into a ponytail, and headed out for a jog through the cityscape.

The cool morning air felt good in her lungs.

She got into a rhythm and picked up the pace, doing five-minute kilometers, or better.

She tried to not think of Hong Kong, but it had been popping into her thoughts more and more frequently since her father got murdered.

That was one week ago, exactly.

Last Tuesday.

He was shot in the back of the head by a fare,

someone who didn't mind splattering someone else's brains all over the windshield of a cab for a few measly euros.

Hong Kong.
She had buried the memory at one point, but it came back in the last few days. It happened six months ago, when she was in the middle of her second year of graduate work at the University of Hong Kong.
On a Saturday night, she went clubbing; her and Ushi.
They wore expensive high heels and skimpy clothes that showed off curvy bodies.
They drank.
They drank some more.
The men started to look good.
Then something happened.
A man walked over, put his arms around her and kissed her like he owned her. He was six foot, with a rough bad-boy look and long black hair. She cocked her arm back to slap him, but before she could, he pulled her onto the dance floor.
What happened next wasn't clear.
She remembered dancing.
Groping.
Drinking.
Kissing.
Laughing.
She remembered wanting to screw his brains out.
Maybe that happened.

Maybe it didn't.

She couldn't remember.

What she did remember was waking up in a windowless room with a serious headache. She was kept prisoner there for two weeks. She had contact with only one person, a man who always wore a black hood. She had no idea who he was, but he wasn't the bad-boy from the club.

His body was different.

His voice was different.

His everything was different.

She wasn't mistreated.

Then one day, out of the blue, she was released.

It came with a warning, a crystal clear warning; *get out of Hong Kong by midnight and never tell anyone what happened.*

She flew out of Hong Kong at 11:45 p.m. that night and returned to Paris.

She told no one, not even her father, who quit his job at Musee d'Orsay four months after she got back and became a cab driver. That's what he was doing last week—driving a cab—when someone put a bullet in the back of his head and took his money.

A hundred euros, max, according to police estimates.

Probably only half that.

Two hours after her jog, she was drinking coffee and studying at a sidewalk table on Rue de Montmartra when a woman sat down and said, "I'm Emmanuelle Laurent."

Prarie studied her, expecting to know her from somewhere.

But she didn't and said, "Prarie Dubois."

"I know."

The woman was a few inches taller and slightly older than Prarie—twenty-six or twenty-seven—with a tight body and a sensuous face built to break hearts. She wore loose khaki pants, a pink tank top and a stylish lightweight jacket.

She had no makeup.

Long blond hair cascaded down her back, very sexy even by Paris standards.

"I'd like to show you something," Emmanuelle said. Prarie must have had confusion on her face because the woman added, "It's at Musee d'Orsay."

Musee d'Orsay?

That was where her father worked for more than twenty years, in the preservation department, before mysteriously quitting two months ago to take a job as a taxi driver. The museum was world renowned for its impressionist paintings.

Van Gogh.

Renoir.

Degas.

Pissarro.

Monet.

"Why? What's at Musee d'Orsay?"

"You'll see," Emmanuelle said.

4

August 4
Tuesday Morning

Kong lived on an Island Packet 35 sailboat that he moored in the Causeway Bay Typhoon Shelter of Hong Kong and only took out when the water got mean enough to kill him. The rest of the time, the bluewater vessel remained in the marina.

The boat was the perfect size.

It was big enough to accommodate his six-foot frame.

It was small enough that he could handle it on his own.

It was built for screwing.

It was also built for heavy weather, meaning it could roll completely over and self-right without taking on water. He knew, because he had done exactly that, twice. The second time snapped the mast. That was an inconvenience, a story for telling at the club but not much more.

The boat was nice but it wasn't his passion.

Money was his passion, money and women.

He was built to excel at both. At 31-years-old, he owned a perfect body ripped with muscles, hazel eyes, flawless skin, a face that turned women into disposable pleasures, and thick black rock star hair that hung past his shoulders.

He had money, even by Hong Kong standards.

He didn't flaunt it and, in fact, worked hard at keeping a low profile. Men noticed him, but women noticed him even more. For most, he was nothing more than a fleeting vision, eye candy passing by on the street. For others, however, for the perfect ones, the special one percent, he actually became candy that he let them taste.

Some were single.

Some were married.

He didn't discriminate.

He was born and raised in Shanghai, but stayed on the island after getting a graduate degree at the University of Hong Kong in economics—a degree that he had never used and never would, but was still glad he had. He fluently spoke both of Hong Kong's official languages—Cantonese and English—but also got by in Spanish and Japanese.

He woke up shortly before noon on Tuesday, stretched, slipped into trunks, headed topside and dove into the water. Then he swam out of the marina and straight out into Victoria Harbour for half an hour before turning around and heading back.

Mid-afternoon, his phone rang and a surprise voice came through.

"It's me," the woman said.

The voice belonged to his blackmailer.

Kong's chest tightened.

"We're done," he said. "No more."

"I wish we were," she said. "I don't like this any more than you do."

Kong rang his fingers through his hair.

"Here are your choices," he said. "Hang up the phone, right now, and live; or wish you had, later, when I find out who you are—which I will."

The woman chuckled.

"Same amount and same place as before," she said. "Five o'clock tomorrow."

The line went dead.

Kong closed the phone and threw it at a seagull with all his might.

The bird's skull shattered with a pop.

5

August 4
Tuesday Morning

Tuesday morning, Teffinger's alarm clock jerked him out of a fitful sleep with all the subtleness of a freight train. He took a three-mile jog, showered and got to the office just as dawn broke, well before anyone else. Working was impossible. Instead, he paced next to the windows, propped himself up with caffeine and nervously second-guessed the sanity of everything he did last night.

He may well have ruined his life.

Time would tell.

The only certain thing was that he couldn't go back and undo it.

Sydney Heatherwood showed up shortly after seven, wearing a white blouse that looked extra crisp against her African American skin. Teffinger personally stole her out of the vice unit a year ago. Although she was only twenty-seven and still the newbie of the homicide unit, she had already cut her teeth on some of Denver's worst.

John Ganjon.

Nathan Wickerfield.

Jack Draven.

Aaron Trane.

Dylan Jekker.

Trent Tripp.

She got coffee, took a seat in one of the worn leather chairs in front of Teffinger's desk and said, "What's wrong?"

"Nothing."

"Something's wrong, I can tell."

"Nothing's wrong."

She stood up, gave him a sideways glance and said, "Fine, be that way."

The call Teffinger had been dreading came mid-morning. A body had been found next to a BNSF railroad spur on the north edge of the city. The victim was a woman, an Asian woman, about thirty, with a wound to her chest.

Teffinger jotted down the information, swung by Sydney's desk and said, "You feel like taking a ride?"

She looked up.

"A body?"

He nodded.

"It sounds like the same place we found Angela Pfeiffer."

She grunted.

"Now there's a name from the past."

They spent three hours processing the scene. On the drive back, Teffinger knew he shouldn't do what he was about to do. It would put Sydney in a precarious position but telling her was necessary.

The Beatles' "Thank You Girl" came from the Tundra's radio.

Teffinger punched it off and said, "I need to tell you something."

Sydney put a shocked look on her face.

"You just turned off a Beatles song," she said.

"Yeah, I know."

"You spend most of your waking moments trying to find a Beatles song."

That was true.

"I knew something was wrong," she said.

Teffinger exhaled.

"I've been debating whether I should tell you what I'm about to tell you," he said. "I finally concluded that it would be wrong to do it but more wrong not to do it, so here it goes." He told her about last night— he came home to find a woman sitting on his front steps in the rain; she was a model from Hong Kong named d'Asia who was running for her life; Teffinger said he'd help her; someone showed up in the middle of the night and tried to kill her; she ended up wrestling the knife away from her attacker and killing her in self defense; then she disappeared into the storm.

Sydney frowned.

"Nothing's ever normal with you Teffinger," she said. "At least tell me you didn't fall in love with this woman."

Teffinger said nothing.

"God, I can't believe you sometimes."

Teffinger grunted.

"You've done this a thousand times, Nick," she said. "You meet a woman and—bam!—everything else in the universe disappears."

"There's more to the story," Teffinger said.

"More?"

"It gets worse," Teffinger said. "I should have called the Lakewood P.D. but I didn't," he said. "Instead I had a couple of more beers. Then I did something stupid. I put the body in the back of my truck, threw a tarp over it and dumped it by some railroad tracks. The scene that you and I just investigated is the woman from last night."

Sydney stared at him.

"You're messing with me, right?"

No.

He wasn't.

"I don't get it," she said. "Why? Why would do such a crazy thing? There was a homicide at your house. You tampered with it on purpose. You moved a body. That goes against every rule in the universe."

Teffinger nodded.

He knew that.

"It's not something I did lightly."

"Lightly, heavily, what's the difference?" Sydney said. "It's insane. You could lose your job. No, not could, will."

Teffinger didn't disagree.

"Here's the way I look at it," he said. "If I called Lakewood, they'd chalk it up as self-defense—which it was—and close the case. I'd never find out who the woman was, much less who she works for. So I moved the body to Denver to get the case under my jurisdiction. If I'm the investigating officer, the Hong Kong authorities will cooperate with me. I'm not only going to find out who she was, but who she was working for. That's the only way I can help d'Asia."

Sydney shook her head in disbelief.

"So you put your entire career on the line to help some stranger?"

Silence.

Then Teffinger said, "I promised her. This was the only way I could figure out how to do it." A pause, then he added, "But I'll admit there's more than that. I need to find her and get her in my life." He squeezed Sydney's hand. "I'm sorry to lay this on you, but I couldn't have you wasting time on the case. Plus you have a right to know, on a personal level."

She shook her head.

"I'm not going to tell anyone," she said. "But between you and me, you went too far. You've always been on the edge, we both know that, but this is too much, even for you."

Teffinger exhaled.

"I promised her," he said.

"That's not an excuse."

"I know," he said. "But when you strip away all the peripherals in life, all you really have is your word."

6

August 4
Tuesday Morning

Musee D'Orsay sat on the right bank of the Seine and protected the world's greatest collection of impressionistic art from the elements. Prarie started going there at age four, when her father used to bring her to work, and even then understood there was something timelessly special about the colors and brushstrokes and vibrancy of the paintings that her father referred to as "his babies." "Not like you though," he always added. "You're more special than everything in here put together."

Really?

Really.

"All of Paris, even."

Normally she felt a sense of exhilaration and awe when she went there. The paintings always energized her and deepened her and expanded her. This time, however, walking to the entrance with some stranger named Emmanuelle Laurent at her side, she didn't feel any of that.

She felt serious, as if her life was about to change.

"What I'm going to tell you and show you must remain confidential," Emmanuelle said. "You must give me your word that whether you decide to help me or not, you won't tell anyone what I'm about to tell you."

Help her?

What did that mean?

"I don't understand what's going on," Prarie said.

"You will."

Five minutes later they were standing in front of Claude Monet's "Poppies," which depicted women with hats strolling through a green field with red flowers. A line of dark trees on the horizon separated the field from a summer sky.

"Have you ever seen this painting before?" Emmanuelle asked.

Prarie nodded.

"About a hundred times."

"A hundred times?"

"Right."

"Do you like it?"

"Sure. Who wouldn't?"

"What do you like about it?"

Prarie shrugged. "I don't understand what's going on."

"Just indulge me for a moment," Emmanuelle said. "Look at the painting carefully and tell me what you like about it." Prarie almost protested, enough was enough, but studied the painting.

"I don't know … the colors, the composition, the brushstrokes—everything," she said. "There's no part of it I don't like."

"I agree," Emmanuelle said. "It's nice. There's only one thing wrong with it, that I can tell."

"What's that?"

Emmanuelle looked around to be sure she wouldn't be overheard, then whispered in Prarie's ear, "It's a fake." Prarie must have had a look on her face as if she was about to repeat the words out loud, because Emmanuelle put her finger on Prarie's lips and said, "Shhh."

No.

That wasn't possible.

"This painting has been authenticated a hundred times," she said.

"Not in the last six months it hasn't," Emmanuelle said. "Want to see some more fakes?"

Prarie did.

She did indeed.

Emmanuelle took her to see four more paintings.

Van Gogh's "Self Portrait."

August Renoir's "Nude in the Sunlight."

Edgar Degas' "Absinthe."

Edouard Manet's "At the Beach."

Prarie had seen each of these paintings before, many times before, spanning a period of years. They were exactly as she remembered them, right down to the faded colors, the textures, the paint over paint and the time begotten cracks. Not a one of them looked less than a hundred percent authentic or an iota different than she remembered.

Why did the woman think they were fakes?

Why did she care?

And why was she was bothering to tell any of this to Prarie?

She was just about to ask these questions when Emmanuelle grabbed her hand and led her towards the exit. "Let's go outside where we can talk. I have to warn you in advance, though. This is going to be a little unsettling."

"Unsettling how?"

"You'll see in a minute," she said. "Just be prepared."

7

August 4
Tuesday Morning

Prarie and Emmanuelle ended up on the cobblestone walkway next to the Seine. A Batobus carved a wake as it motored east and passed a slow-moving barge. The Parisian sun sparkled on the water. A seagull flew low over the river, warding off other gulls who were trying to steal something out of its mouth.

Survival of the fittest; it was everywhere, at every level, all the time.

"Okay, here's the thing," Emmanuelle said. "The five paintings I showed you—the original five paintings—were stolen from the museum six months ago and the fakes were substituted in their place at that time. The museum found out about it two months ago. It made a number of insurance claims. The CIM Group is the primary insurer for the museum, covering the first $200,000,000 in loss. There are excess insurance carriers behind CIM who are also on the hook. I've been retained by CIM in an ad hoc capacity to find the paintings. Technically, I'm an independent contractor, which gives me the flexibility to bend the law if I need to without getting CIM in trouble. No one knows who I'm working for and I need you to keep it that way. Will you?"

Prarie shrugged.

Sure.

Why not?

"Very few people know about this," Emmanuelle said. "The fakes are extraordinarily accurate. They're good enough that the museum is letting them hang until the matter can be resolved one way or the other."

A teenage girl with too much makeup strolled past.

"I still don't understand what any of this has to do with me," Prarie said.

Emmanuelle exhaled.

"Here's what happened as far as we can tell so far," Emmanuelle said. "Someone did some research and found out who key museum employees were. They found out who worked in the preservation department."

"That's where my father worked," Prarie said.

Emmanuelle nodded.

"Unfortunately, yes, your father," she said. "They also found out who worked in the security department, which was headed by a man named Yves Blanc."

Prarie didn't recognize the name.

"I don't know him," she said.

"No reason you would," Emmanuelle said. "Anyway, your father had a daughter, namely you. The head of the security department, Yves Blanc, also had a daughter, namely an 8-year-old named Dominique Blanc."

Prarie chewed her lip, dreading the words to come.

"Your father, being in the preservation department, had access to all the paintings," Emmanuelle said. "If he got motivated enough, and if security worked with him, he'd be able to get original paintings off the walls, into his department, and out the door. He'd also be able to get fakes hung in their place. All he needed was to be motivated enough. He got that motivation when you were kidnapped in Hong Kong."

Now it made sense, perfect sense, finally after all this time.

"After they took you, they contacted your father and gave him an ultimatum," Emmanuelle said. "They also contacted the head of security, Yves Blanc, and told him that both you and his daughter would die if he didn't cooperate in the plan."

Prarie cocked her head.

"So they never actually took the 8-year-old?"

Emmanuelle shook her head.

"No, they didn't have to," she said. "Taking you made it real enough to make Yves Blanc cooperate. The rest is pretty straightforward. The paintings were switched while you were held captive. Afterwards, they let you go."

"I had no idea," Prarie said.

Emmanuelle squeezed her hand.

"Your father stole art to save your life," Emmanuelle said. "Unfortunately, it gets worse."

"Everything went undetected for about four months," Emmanuelle said. "Then one of the paintings—the Monet—was going to be shown in a special exhibit in London. Of course, whenever that happens, the piece is inspected by both the museum and the accepting party. That's when it was discovered to be a fake. Over the next month, every painting in the museum was inspected, which lead to the discovery of the other four fakes. A lot of people did a lot of brainstorming about what happened and came up with the theory that I just told you."

"What did my father have to say about it?" Prarie asked.

"Nothing," Emmanuelle said. "He wouldn't cooperate. Neither would Yves Blanc. They both denied having any knowledge or involvement, no doubt because they had been threatened that you would be killed if they ever cooperated with the police."

"And the 8-year-old too, I assume," Prarie added.

"Of course," Emmanuelle said. "They were both protecting the lives of their daughters. The museum had no alternative but to discharge both of them. That's why your father left the museum and took a job as a taxi driver. He didn't quit, he was fired. He was a good man. He did what he did but he also had no choice. Everyone who knows about the situation agrees that they would have done the same thing in his position. No one blames him. They didn't want to fire him, but couldn't keep him on for obvious reasons. Everyone at the museum was very clear in that they would never file criminal charges against him. That's why he never got arrested." She sighed. "Unfortunately, it might have been better if he had."

Prarie cocked her head.

"What does that mean?"

"It means this," Emmanuelle said. "Word of what happened is getting out. Now, unfortunately, there is at least one group of people, and maybe more, who know the paintings are out there in the world somewhere and are hunting for them—not to return them, but for their own personal wealth. It's our belief that one of those groups confronted your father to try to get a lead. Your father didn't cooperate. They shot him in the back of the head and made it look like a routine robbery."

Prarie pictured it and shivered.

"Yves Blanc was also killed last week," Emmanuelle said. "Did you know that?"

No.

She didn't.

"It gets worse," Emmanuelle said. "With your father and Yves Blanc now gone, there's only one connection left to the original robbers, namely you. That's why I'm seeking you out and why they will be, too."

"But I don't know anything," Prarie said.

"Maybe yes, maybe no," Emmanuelle said. "What I propose is that you and I go to Hong Kong and find out. We'll try to get a lead based on what you know about your own kidnapping. Don't worry about money. I'll cover everything."

DAY FOUR

August 6
Thursday

8

August 6
Thursday Morning

A raven-haired flight attendant with white teeth sat down next to Teffinger an hour into the flight, looked into his eyes, and said, "I thought that's what I saw. They're two different colors. One's blue and one's green."

He nodded.

"I like to wear my flaws up front," he said. "That way no one gets surprised down the road."

She chuckled.

"You don't look like you have too many flaws."

Her name turned out to be Ling Ling.

She lived in Hong Kong.

She ended up sitting next to Teffinger more than she should.

She told him about Hong Kong.

"Hong Kong is a hurricane, a big powerful un-stoppable hurricane, blowing at full force, all day and all night. Everything you want is there somewhere, every earthly pleasure and every earthly sin." She cocked her head. "Personally, I like the sins better, myself."

He smiled.

"That sounds reasonable."

"I'll show you Hong Kong, if you want," she said. "I'm not talking about the buildings and the streets and the restaurants. I'm talking about the real Hong Kong, the one under the clothes."

"Under the clothes, huh?"

She ran a finger across his hand.

"Yes, the secret Hong Kong."

The flight got in just as the sun broke over the horizon. Surprisingly, from the sky, the place actually did look like a hurricane. The eye of that hurricane, namely the sci-fi skyscrapers of Hong Kong's central business district, sat on the north edge of Hong Kong Island, sandwiched between a mountain range to the south and the blue waters of Victoria Harbour to the north. That was the no-nonsense hunting ground of the rich and powerful, where top dollar and bottom lines ruled. Across the water to the north, a short ferry ride away, sat the bustling Kowloon district, given to shopping, hotels, apartment complexes, neon signs and crazy traffic.

Teffinger felt his pulse race.

Ling Ling gave him her number and told him to call.

"I will," he said.

"Promise," she said.

He hesitated and then said, "I promise."

She ran a finger over his lips.

"Don't break your promise, Nick Teffinger," she said.

"I won't."

"Are you sure?"

He nodded.

"I have a lot of flaws, but that's not one of them."

They kissed, just a taste, and parted.

Outside, Teffinger stuck his head in a cab and said, "Do you know where a hotel called the Fleming is?"

A 60-year-old face grinned.

"Yeah, but I'm going to pretend like I don't and drive around and run the meter up, if that's okay with you."

Teffinger grinned.

"Honesty," he said. "I like that. What's your name?"

"Butch."

"Butch?"

"Right, Butch."

"You look Chinese."

"That's probably because both my parents are Chinese and because I was born here."

Butch told Teffinger a few things about the lay of the land. Although he'd hear plenty of Cantonese—which was a southern Chinese dialect—almost everyone spoke English too, very good English in fact. English signs almost universally accompanied their Chinese counterparts. Lots of the locals went by a western name in addition to their formal Chinese name.

Johnny.

Lilly.

Jack.

Currency was in Hong Kong dollars (HKD), with the current exchange rate being seven-to-one. ATMs were everywhere and plastic got whipped out of wallets faster than dicks at a whore house. Bottom line—Teffinger would be able to function without much of a problem.

"What about coffee?" Teffinger asked. "Tell me there's coffee."

"Coffee?"

"Right."

"No, no coffee here," Butch said. "Coffee is not good for you. We drink mostly prune juice."

Teffinger must have had a look on his face because Butch busted into laughter and added, "Got you."

"Got me?"

"Right, got you."

"So there is coffee, right? Just to be sure I'm getting this straight."

Butch nodded.

"More than you could drink in a thousand years."

Teffinger grunted.

"You've never seen me drink."

The Fleming turned out to be an upscale boutique hotel near Causeway Bay just east of the business district on Hong Kong Island. Teffinger gave Butch a more than fair tip, checked into the cheapest room available and then headed to the Metro under a hazy humid sky to meet his contact, a detective—someone named Fan Rae Fan.

9

August 6
Thursday Morning

Prarie and Emmanuelle landed at Hong Kong International Airport shortly before noon on Thursday and took a red taxi to the InterContinental Hotel, which was an insanely over-the-top Kowloon hotel on the north side of Victoria Harbour, literally resting on stilts over the water.

It was expensive but secure.

They checked in under Emmanuelle's name, took the elevator to the fifteenth floor, and stepped into an opulent room furnished with Asian art, rich silks and elegant textures. The spacious bathroom was fitted with Italian marble, a sunken tub and separate shower. High-speed Internet and email access were complimentary. Emmanuelle opened the window coverings. The skyline of Hong Kong loomed large less than two kilometers across the harbour.

"Impressive," she said.

Prarie swallowed.

"I forgot how big it is."

The city looked the same as always, visually, but instead of feeling exciting and adventurous it now felt dangerous and foreboding.

Sinister, even.

"Are you okay?" Emmanuelle asked.

Prarie turned and said, "Yes," but there was no conviction in her voice. "I can't be me here," she added. "I need to change my hair, minimum."

"You think?"

Yeah.

She did.

They unpacked and then headed down to the spa, where Prarie gave a flamboyantly gay man in his late twenties simple instructions—"Make me look different."

"How different?"

"Totally."

The man studied her for ten seconds and said, "You are now in the hands of Park. Stay in the chair until we come to a complete stop." Then he cut off eight inches of blond hair, styled what was left with rapid scissor swipes, and dyed everything black except for one white streak on the right side.

"It looks like something you'd see on the catwalk," Emmanuelle said. "Very nice."

"You think?"

"Definitely."

Prarie studied it in the mirror.

"I've never not been blond before," she said. "I'm going to have to get used to it."

They took the Star Ferry across Victoria Harbour, grabbed a green taxi and headed for the place where Prarie had been released after being held captive for two weeks. They ended up on a deserted road twenty kilometers southeast of the city.

"Right here," Prarie said.

"Stop," Emmanuelle told the cabbie. "We're getting out."

The man wrinkled his brow.

"Here?"

"Yes."

"Are you sure?"

Emmanuelle looked at Prarie, who nodded, and then said, "Yes, what do we owe you?"

She paid. The cab disappeared. They were alone.

Nothing moved.

Not a sound came from anywhere.

"Okay, walk me through it," Emmanuelle said. "Tell me exactly how it worked."

"Okay, I was in the trunk the whole time," Prarie said. "My hands were tied behind my back and there was a black hood over my head. We drove for thirty or forty minutes and ended up stopping right here. The man turned the engine off, got out, came around to the back and opened the trunk. He pulled me out and then cut the ropes off my wrists. I started to raise my hands to take the hood off but he said, No!"

"Okay."

"I froze," Prarie said.

"So would I."

"Then he said, 'I'm going to get in the car and take off. You're going to stand here and keep the blindfold on and count to a hundred, slowly, before you take it off. I'll be watching you in the mirror. If you take it off before you're supposed to, I won't have any choice but to come back. Do you understand?'"

"So, did you do it? Did you keep it on?"

"I wanted to rip it off, because I thought he was going to shoot me," she said. "But I kept it on, just in case he was serious. At that point, all I wanted to do was live. There was no way I was going to give him an excuse to do anything. You can't believe how I felt when he actually got in the car and took off."

Emmanuelle nodded, understanding.

"Which way did he go?"

Prarie pointed and said, "The same way the cab just went."

"And that's the way he came from, right?"

Good question.

"Yes," she said.

"How do you know?"

"Because I remember now, that he turned the car around after he took me out."

"Okay, good."

"I didn't remember that until just now," Prarie said.

"Okay, what happened next?"

"Well, I took off the hood after I got to a hundred," Prarie said. "I looked in the direction the car had gone and couldn't see it. It had already disappeared. I was alone. Then I started walking that way, the same way as the car."

"What did you do with the hood?"

Prarie shrugged.

"I don't remember."

They searched the area and found it in the weeds, plus the rope.

Emmanuelle put them both in her purse.

"Okay, so you started walking that way, right?"

"Right."

"Then what?"

"Eventually, I came to that gas station at the crossroads we passed about three or four kilometers back. The guy there called a cab for me. I took it back to campus, packed a bag and headed for the airport."

"Okay."

"That's it," Prarie said. "That's all there is to it."

They headed up the road.

The sun beat down relentlessly through a humid haze.

"Where the hell are all the cars?" Emmanuelle asked.

"There aren't any," Prarie said. "Welcome to my life."

Emmanuelle chuckled.

"Your life sucks."

"Tell me about it."

A kilometer passed, a hot sweaty one.

"I'd give a hundred euros for a ride right now," Emmanuelle said.

"That's weird that you said that," Prarie said, "because that was the exact thing I was thinking when I was here last time, when a car came up the road going the opposite way. The guy didn't even have the decency to stop and see if I was okay."

"Jerk," Emmanuelle said.

"Exactly."

They walked for another ten minutes, not talking, dealing with the heat.

Then Emmanuelle said, "If I was a man driving out here and saw a woman walking by herself, particularly a blond foreigner, I think I'd be inclined to stop and see what was going on."

"You'd think."

"Maybe he didn't stop because he already knew what was going on."

Prarie tilted her head.

"What does that mean?"

"It means that maybe he already knew who you were because he was the one who dropped you off," Emmanuelle said.

"I don't see the connection."

"Think about it," Emmanuelle said. "If it was him, he wouldn't stop and pretend it wasn't him, because you'd recognize his voice. He'd just keep driving, which is exactly what he did."

That made sense, to a point.

"But why would he double back?"

"Easy," Emmanuelle said. "The quickest way back to where he was going was that way."

"That doesn't make sense. If that's the way he wanted to go, why wouldn't he have just gone that way to begin with?"

"Because he didn't want you to know which way he was really headed. He didn't want you to know that the place you were being kept was somewhere down that road."

Prarie wiped sweat off her forehead.

"The heat's frying your brain," she said.

Emmanuelle ignored the remark and said, "Did you get a look at him?"

"Who? The driver?"

"Right."

"Yeah, for about a tenth of a second, from the side, while he was speeding and I was wiping sweat out of my was eyes and cursing him for not stopping."

"Would you recognize him if you saw him?"

"Are you kidding? No way."

"Do you remember what color the car was?"

"No."

"Do you remember anything?"

"I remember I would have given him a hundred euros," Prarie said. "That's it."

"Okay."

"Sorry."

10

August 6
Thursday Morning

Kong's phone rang Thursday morning and the voice of Jack Poon came through. Kong pulled up the image of a short underweight man who owned more of Hong Kong that any other human being, not even counting the Macau casino. Poon didn't call often, but when he did Kong listened and listened hard, not just because of the man's wealth and power but because he also owned Ra, which Kong managed.

"Do you know how to parachute?" Poon asked.

Parachute?

What the hell?

"I did it once," Kong said.

"Did you live?"

"To the best of my recollection."

Poon chuckled.

"Good. I'd like to meet with you. Do you have time?"

Kong did.

He did indeed.

A 15-meter Predator picked him up an hour later at the marina and sliced through choppy seas at a breakneck pace to Macau, sixty kilometers to the west, where a black Bentley was waiting for him. Fifteen minutes later he was in the penthouse suite of the Cotai Storm Hotel & Casino—one of several places Poon called home.

Poon slapped Kong on the arm and said, "My man Kong. Thanks for coming."

"No problem."

"How's the club?"

"The club is fine. You should come down some time."

"I will, when I can break free. Right now, I want to talk to you about something. Do you feeling like making some money?"

Kong nodded.

"Always."

"Follow me," Poon said. "I want you to meet someone."

They went to the mater bedroom, which was in semi-darkness. Sprawled out on the bed was a beautiful young woman, about 22, deeply unconscious on her back with her legs spread, wearing only a white thong.

Poon walked over, stuck his hand between the woman's legs and rubbed her.

She didn't move, not a muscle.

"This is Fion," Poon said. "I rent her by the day. She won't come to for another five or six hours. You want to play with her?"

Kong shook his head.

"She looks fun," he said, "but that's really not my thing."

"It wasn't mine either," Poon said. "Don't ever get too much money. It twists you."

They went to the game room and Poon put a pinball machine in action. While working the flippers, he looked up and said, "If you can beat me two out of three, I'll tell you what I have in mind."

Kong nodded.

"Fair enough."

11

August 6
Thursday Morning

Fan Rae Fan stared at Teffinger when he walked into her office, not saying anything, just taking him in. He did the same—he had no choice, he really couldn't form words, not quite yet. She reminded him a lot of d'Asia, but was slightly taller and even more stunning, if that was possible. Her hair was long, straight and pitch-black. Until this moment, he thought he came to Hong Kong not just to help d'Asia, but to get her into his life.

Now he was confused, just like that.

Wham.

"You must be Nick Teffinger," the woman said. Her English was remarkably good, with just a trace of Asian overlay.

"Guilty."

"Someone named Sydney Heatherwood called me this morning," she said. "She told me the secret."

"The secret?"

"Right. The secret is the coffee. Too little, and things aren't right with you. Too much, and more of the same. The secret is to get the perfect balance."

Teffinger smiled.

"There's no such thing as too much," he said. "What else did she tell you?"

Fan Rae pulled an imaginary zipper across her lips.

"Nothing I can repeat but don't worry, I only believe half of it."

"Which half? The good one or the bad one?"

"There's a good half?" she said. "Follow me."

They got coffee from a small kitchenette down the hall.

That gave him a chance to see how she walked.

He wasn't disappointed.

As soon as they got back to her office, the phone rang. She talked in quick Cantonese and increasingly wrinkled her brow.

"Got a homicide," she said. "You want to tag along or wait until I get back?"

"I'll tag."

They got into a small silver vehicle and pointed the nose east into thick traffic.

"I ran the prints of your Denver victim and didn't get any matches," Fan Rae said. "I also showed her photo around. No one recognizes her and no matches are popping up in the database."

"So you have no idea who she is?"

"Not yet," she said. "Tell me again why you think she's from Hong Kong."

"We found Hong Kong dollars in her pocket."

"Oh, right. I forgot."

"By the way, thanks for all your trouble, I really appreciate it."

She nodded, understanding.

"You can't find the killer until you know who the victim is," she said.

"Still, thanks."

Twenty minutes later they were at a secluded beach. Two uniforms directed them to a body. The victim turned out to be a g-punk woman in her mid-twenties, with black hair, heavy black makeup, multiple piercings and a tongue stud.

She was staked out in the sand.

Naked.

Tight.

Nothing was around her.

No clothes.

No purse.

No nothing.

Only her.

Her throat was slit.

Deep.

But that wasn't the weird part.

The weird part was her stomach.

Someone had carved markings into her flesh. From the flow of the blood, it was obviously done while she was still alive. Teffinger swallowed and momentarily got distracted by the waves crashing on the sand.

Fan Rae said, "That's a K'ung chia symbol. It means bad or evil or vicious."

"Meaning her?"

"No," she said. "No, not her. It refers to the carver."

12

August 6
Thursday Afternoon

The man behind the counter at the gas station gave Prarie a long sideways look as if he'd seen her before, but said nothing. She and Emmanuelle made their way back to the hotel, showered, rented a VW Passat and drove from one art gallery to another. "I want to commission a Monet replica," Emmanuelle said. "Do you know anyone who does that kind of work?"

"No."

That was the standard answer.

No.

No, no, no.

Until they stopped at a gallery in the low rent district in northern Kowloon. There, a bald man with thick black glasses named Quon said, "How good of a replica are you looking for?"

"A perfect one."

"A perfect one?"

"Right, as in identical."

"That would be difficult with a Monet," Quon said. "The colors are layered—you're talking paint on paint on paint. Plus you'd have to age it."

"I know."

"Something like that would be pricey."

"Does that mean you know someone?"

The man laughed.

"Me? No, but there are rumors—," he said. "I can make some phone calls, if you want. There would be a charge for that, of course, and there aren't any guarantees."

She gave him a $1,000 HKD.

"I'll call you tomorrow," she said.

Outside, Prarie said, "I don't trust that guy."

"Good. That will keep you alive."

Emmanuelle fired u the engine and said, "Let's get back to the hotel and take a nap. It's going to be a long night."

Prarie pictured it and frowned.

She almost said, I'm still not sure I can do it.

Instead she said, "Good idea."

13

August 6
Thursday Afternoon

When Jack Poon told Kong what he wanted him to do, Kong's first thought was that it would be scary, but he could handle it, including the parachute jump. His second thought was that Poon was one sick son-of-a-bitch, seriously twisted.

The money had warped him.

He hadn't been strong enough to handle it.

Worse, if what Poon said was true, there were others like him; several in fact.

Kong kept all emotion off his face and said, "Sounds doable."

"So you're in?"

Kong nodded.

"Of course."

Poon slapped him on the back and said, "I'll set it up for tomorrow. It goes without saying, of course, that you never mention a word of this to anyone, even ten years from now."

"Don't worry."

Five minutes later, as he was about to leave, Kong said over his shoulder, "Why me?"

"What do you mean?"

"Why did you choose me for this assignment?"

"Maybe it's a test, to see what you got."

"I got plenty."

"We'll see."

By the time Kong got back to the marina, he had a few things settled in his mind. He needed to do well on this assignment and then cultivate a relationship with Poon. He also needed to get Poon to introduce him to the others. If he could get three or four Poons in his life, he'd be set—not that he wasn't set already, but there were different degrees of set.

A surprise was waiting for him at the sailboat, namely Kam Lee Yao in a white bikini with the top untied, lying on her stomach in the shade of the canopy. Her body dripped from a fresh swim.

Kong straddled her ass and rubbed her back.

"This is unexpected," he said. "Business or pleasure?"

She rolled over, pulled the top to the side and stretched her arms up.

"Pleasure."

Kong teased her nipples.

Then he took her below and screwed her hard, until she made those little sounds that he loved so much.

Afterwards he said, "What do you know about a guy named Jack Poon?"

She studied him, visibly surprised by the question.

"Jack Poon?"

"Right."

"I know he has money," she said. "Why? What's going on?"

"I might have a chance to get in good with him," Kong said.

"With Jack Poon? Really—"

Kong nodded.

"How?"

"I can't say," Kong said. "Has he ever been to your establishment?"

She smiled.

"Establishment? Is that what you called it?"

Kong grinned.

"Yeah, I guess I did."

"No," she said. "He's never been to my establishment. But it's time for you to. I want you to do a session with me."

Kong slapped her ass.

"I just did a session with you."

"You know what I mean."

Yes.

He did.

He did indeed.

"I'll think about it."

She put a serous look on her face and said, "Be careful of Poon."

"Why?"

"I've heard rumors, that's all."

"Like what?"

"Like it's not very healthy to get on his bad side."

Kong kissed her and said, "I might need your help."

"How?"

He shrugged.

"I don't know yet," he said. "If I do, though, can I count on you?"

"You already know the answer to that."

14

August 6
Thursday Afternoon

Fan Rae and Teffinger worked the murder scene without much interference for thirty minutes. Then more and more people showed up, including an older man, well dressed, who threw Teffinger sideways looks and spoke in jagged Cantonese to Fan Rae. She walked over two minutes later and said, "That's my boss. I just got chewed out for letting you on the crime scene."

"Sorry."

"It's not your fault," she said. "It's mine."

Two news helicopters appeared overhead.

Teffinger focused on them, momentarily distracted, and then said, "Did you smell the victim?"

"Smell her? No—"

"Go take a whiff," he said. "She's got perfume on her neck and on her thighs. Also, her hair has lots of cigarette smoke in it. I don't think it's from her. Her teeth don't show any nicotine staining. And there's no smell of smoke on her fingers, like you'd find if she'd been holding cigarettes."

Fan Rae checked it out, then added it to her report.

"So what do you make of it?" she asked.

"I've been to a bar or two in my day," Teffinger said. "That's how I smelled the next morning. I'm guessing we're going to find alcohol in her stomach."

"So maybe someone saw who she left with," Fan Rae said.

Teffinger shrugged.

"You never know."

Fan Rae studied him and said, "You know that guy who just chewed me out? He never comes up with stuff like that." She leaned in and whispered, "So screw him."

Teffinger's cell phone rang. He checked the number since it would be an international call if he answered—Sydney Heatherwood.

"Sydney," he said. "What's going on?"

"I just wanted to hear the sound of your voice."

"Bullshit."

"Yeah, bullshit," she said. "Actually there's been a development involving our dead railroad woman. We got a phone call a half hour ago by a man named Randy Rocco. He owns a bar called the Mile High Dogface. You ever heard of it?"

No.

He hadn't.

"Everything's Mile High," he said.

"Anyway," Sydney said, "from what he told me, it's one of little hole in the wall places, close to the tracks. He has a security camera for the parking lot, but it also picks up the road. He heard about the Asian woman's murder and checked his tapes, just for grins. Apparently they show a white pickup truck going down the road towards the tracks in the middle of the night and then leaving the opposite way about ten minutes later. He was all excited on the phone, saying stuff like, It's gotta be the killer!"

She paused.

"I'm on my way over there right now to look at the tapes," she said. "The question is this—what do I do?"

Teffinger knew what she meant, he knew *exactly* what she meant, but he said, "What do you mean?"

"I mean, what if they show your face or license plate number or something—"

Teffinger exhaled and kicked the sand.

"Look," he said, "what I did is my problem, not yours."

"I know, but—"

"No buts," Teffinger said. "I did something stupid. It may end up taking me down. It probably should take me down, if the world works right. But you're not part of it and the worst thing that could happen to me right now is for you to get dirty on my account. So don't do it, you hear me? Just don't do it. I'm serious."

Silence.

Then Sydney said, "How am I supposed to just sit

by and let you go down?"

"I don't care about going down," he said. "I don't even have the right to care about it. I lost that right when I did what I did. But I do care about you going down. So if you're thinking about burying the tapes or losing them or something like that, then tell me right now, because in that case I'm going to call Double-F as soon as I hang up and tell him what I did."

Silence.

"So what do I do?"

"Take the guy's statement, get the tapes, bag 'em as evidence and make 'em part of the file, exactly like you'd do in any other investigation," he said.

Sydney said nothing.

Neither did Teffinger.

Then Sydney said, "Here's the thing. You're the best detective this city has ever had. If it wasn't for you, there'd be lots of people running around on the streets that shouldn't be. I'm the only person in the world who has a chance to keep you in your position."

"Sydney, listen to me," Teffinger said. "I've taught you a lot of stuff over the last year. Now I'm going to teach you one more thing. Don't get dirty. That's your next lesson. Don't get dirty. Period. End of sentence. You've never let me down before. Not once. Don't do it this time."

Silence.

"I want your promise," Teffinger said.

Silence.

Then she said, "Okay."

"Okay what?"

"Okay I promise."

"Thank you. Now go get those tapes."

He must have had a look on his face as he hung up because Fan Rae walked over and said, "Is everything okay?"

He picked up a handful of sand and let it fall through his fingers, then looked at her—no, not at her, into her eyes, way into her eyes.

"I put someone in a bad position," he said. "If she's not strong enough to deal with it, it's going to end up being the worst thing I ever did."

"She?"

"Yes."

"Someone you love?"

He considered it.

"Yes, but not romantically," he said. "A colleague. I need a drink. You want to go somewhere tonight and get a drink?"

She shrugged.

"Sure, if you want."

15

August 6
Thursday Night

Thursday night, Prarie and Emmanuelle bought dresses with designer labels and headed to SoHo, South of Hollywood Boulevard, where the serious clubbing was. The neon streets were mobbed with bar-hopping party animals, dressed to get past the velvet ropes. "I've only seen this much buzz at one other place before," Emmanuelle said. "That was in Bangkok, in the Soi Cowboy district. Have you ever been there?"

"No, Europe and Hong Kong, that's it," Prarie said.

"Go there some time."

"Right."

They ended up at a club called D-Drop, a dark monolithic warehouse space with high-energy DJ's and seriously cool lights, already jammed to the walls.

Sex.

Sex.

Sex.

That's what it was there for.

They ordered screwdrivers, paid a lot, but also got three shots in each glass. Then they muscled through the crowd, looking at the faces.

The plan was simple.

This is where Prarie had been clubbing the night she got taken. The rock star probably slipped something into her drink, meaning he was connected to the people they were looking for.

The hope was that he'd be a regular and Prarie would bump into him by blind luck.

Twenty minutes into it, Emmanuelle said, "I wish I could help."

"He's tall and serious hot," Prarie said.

"I know. You already told me that."

"Long, straight, black hair."

"That's half the guys in here," Emmanuelle said. "Does he have any tattoos?"

"No."

Ten minutes passed.

Drunk faces came and went.

No rock star emerged.

Then Prarie said, "When you asked me about the tattoos, something nagged me. I just figured out what."

"Yeah? What?"

"You asked me before if I got a look at the guy in the car, the guy who passed me after I got released on the road we went to this afternoon. I said I didn't see him. But now I remember something, he had a tattoo on his neck."

"A tattoo?"

"Right."

"You sure?"

"Positive."

"A tattoo of what?"

"I have no idea," Prarie said. "All I remember is that it was prominent and colorful."

Emmanuelle slapped her on the back.

"Way to go, girlfriend. Come on, I owe you a drink for that."

They hunted until their legs screamed and then hovered at the bar until they were able to grab chairs. They fought off men for a half hour and then Prarie said, "Oh my God!"

Emmanuelle followed the woman's eyes.

She followed them to a tall man, a tall muscular man with long straight black hair and a rock star face.

Totally GQ.

Built for sex.

"Is that him?"

Prarie studied the man harder.

"I'm not positive," she said, "but I think so."

The man ordered a beer and disappeared into the crowd.

"Okay," Emmanuelle said, "you get out of here so he doesn't see you. Take a cab back to the hotel. I'll meet you there."

"What are you going to do?"

"I'm going to find out who he is."

Prarie took a cab halfway back, then got a bad feeling and returned to the club. She walked around for an hour and couldn't find Emmanuelle or the rock star.

There wasn't a sign of either of them.

She was just about to leave when an attractive man in a crisp white shirt grabbed her hand and led her to a roped-off area with four or five men and an equal number of women.

Pretty people.

Big jewelry.

White smiles.

One of the women kissed her on the cheek, handed her a drink and said, "Well aren't you the sexy one?"

16

August 6
Thursday Evening

Thursday evening the shadows got long but the air stayed tropical. Teffinger jogged for two sweaty miles, showered, slipped into his best clothes and took the Metro to Fan Rae's apartment, which was on the near west side in a nice but not over-the-top area He bypassed the elevators, walked up five flights of stairs and knocked on 506.

Then he held his breath.

Fan Rae opened the door.

Gone was her professional daytime look. She now had a short white dress, cleavage, high heels, makeup, lots of golden skin and a tiny tattoo of a flower on her shoulder. Her hair hung long and loose and freshly washed. She dangled a wineglass in her left hand, half empty.

Teffinger had never wanted a woman so much in his life.

Well, that wasn't true—he had, but right now they

didn't count.

"I didn't know if you'd come," she said.

"How could I not?"

Her apartment was small, but clean, bright and contemporary, with lots of windows, a balcony and great views. "Come on, I'll show you Hong Kong," she said. "Do you want to see the high-class Hong Kong or the raw and edgy one?"

He didn't hesitate.

"Raw and edgy."

"Good. That's the one I know better."

She linked her arm through his.

Then they headed into the night.

The next couple of hours were a blur. They ate ramen at a noisy, rough-and-ready place where Fan Rae knew everyone by name and the food showed up two minutes after they ordered. Then they headed for the bars in the high energy, sin laden Lan Kwai Foog district.

Kiss.

Joe Bananas.

Club '97.

They all carried Bud Light but Teffinger drank the local stuff.

They got drunk and grabby.

Fan Rae liked to be touched.

She liked it a lot.

The insane heat of the day finally dissipated and Teffinger said, "You know what I could go for?"

She kissed him.

"No, what?"

"Some quiet time, down by the water, someplace dark where the waves break."

"I know a place."

They took a green taxi and ended up on a dark, deserted beach, walking in warm water with bare feet in squishy sand. The lights of Kowloon shimmied to the north and threw a warm patina onto the bellies of low-lying clouds.

The temperature was perfect—about 70.

Fan Rae was perfect.

Everything was perfect.

"Tell me a secret," Fan Rae said. "Tell me something no one else knows about you."

Teffinger was half tempted to play along but slapped her ass and said, "No."

She slapped his ass back.

"Come on," she said. "If you do, I will."

"I don't have any secrets," he said.

"Yes you do, everyone does."

"I'll tell you what I've been thinking about all evening," he said. "How about that?"

She laughed and raised her dress up just long enough to flash a white thong.

"That's not a secret, Teffinger. Come on, be a sport."

"What's my reward, if I play?"

"Whatever you want."

"Whatever I want?"

"Yes, whatever you want."

"Well now you have me interested," he said. "What are my limitations?"

"Only your imagination," she said. "Your imagination and your endurance."

He paused.

"Okay, but I want some payment upfront."

She stood before him.

"Fair enough, what do you want me to do?"

Teffinger led her up to the dry sand, took his shirt off and laid it on the ground. "Take your dress off and lay down on your back," he said.

She did it.

"Wait, take your bra off too."

She leaned up, took the bra off and then plopped back down.

"Raise your arms above your head," he said.

She did it and wiggled her hips.

"It looks like you have me all vulnerable," she said. "But no more, not until you tell me a secret. You can play with my stomach while you talk if you want, but nothing else."

He tweaked her nipples lightly.

"I can't play with these?"

"No, only my stomach."

He ran an index finger in a circle around her bellybutton.

"Like that?"

"Yes, that's fine. Now talk."

Then he did something he didn't think he would do in a million years. He told her about Monday night—how d'Asia had shown up on his front steps asking for his help, and how he gave her a promise. He told her how another woman with a blond wig attacked d'Asia in Teffinger's own bedroom in the middle of the night, and how d'Asia got lucky enough to wrestle the knife away, and ended up killing the woman in self-defense. He told her how d'Asia ran off into the night, to go back to Hong Kong and meet things head on.

He told her how he should have filed a police report.

"But I didn't because I live outside Denver in a city called Lakewood," he said. "If I filed a report with them, they would have chalked it up to self-defense, which it was, and closed the case. That would leave me with no way to fulfill my promise to d'Asia."

So he put the body in his truck and dumped it in Denver next to some railroad tracks.

He got jurisdiction over the case.

"Then I came to Hong Kong, pretending the woman had been killed in my jurisdiction and that I was trying to find out who she was, as a step towards finding out who her killer was," he said. "All that was a lie. Well, not all of it. I am actually trying to find out who she is, but not to find her killer—to get a lead on who she's connected to because that's who's out to kill d'Asia."

He exhaled, not knowing what else to say, waiting for a reaction.

Fan Rae sat up.

"Wow."

"I had no plans to tell you the truth," he said, "until just now. I couldn't let you sleep with me thinking I'm someone I'm not."

She stood up and put her bra on, then her dress.

"That was wrong," she said.

"I know."

They walked in silence.

Then Fan Rae stopped, held Teffinger's hand and said, "Are you in love with this woman? This d'Asia?"

He grunted.

"I came to Hong Kong for two reasons," he said. "One, to help her, because I promised I would; and two, to get her into my life. Then I met you and now I'm confused."

She squeezed his hand.

"I'm going to do something stupid," she said. "I'm going to help you find her."

"Why?"

"Partly so you can fulfill your promise," she said. "But mostly so you can make a choice."

Teffinger tilted his head.

"What does that mean?"

"It means that I don't want to end up with you by default. If I end up with you, I want it to be because you could have had someone else, but affirmatively chose me. I don't want any doubts and I don't want any ghosts."

She took off her dress and dropped it to the sand.

Then her bra.

Then her thong.

Teffinger had never seen a more beautiful woman.

That was the truth.

"That doesn't mean I've fully made up my mind about you," she said.

"I understand."

What happened next wasn't so much sex as it was love.

Tender.

Slow.

Private.

Fan Rae hardly uttered a sound.

Her movements were reserved and calculated, but when she trembled, it was like nothing Teffinger had ever experienced before.

It was like her soul moving into his.

DAY FIVE

August 7
Friday

17

August 7
Friday Morning

Kong got up early Friday morning and checked the sky. What he saw, he didn't like. There were thick black clouds. That, in and of itself, wasn't the problem. The problem was that they were swirling, meaning it wouldn't be a good day to be in a light plane, much less a parachute. He pictured the chute collapsing and trailing above him uselessly as he plunged to earth.

He dived off the boat and swam out of the marina.

The seas were high, on the verge of frothy.

They were dangerous even for him.

He turned around and came back. As soon as he dried off, the phone rang and Jack Poon's voice came though. "Are you still in?"

"Of course."

"Good. Be at the airport at ten, Gate-7. The pilot's a man named Chung Fu Zhang. He's a small man with a gold tooth, about forty. He'll fill you in on all the details. Remember to be convincing. I'm in this to win."

"Understood."

"I'm serious," Poon said. "Scare the living shit out of her."

"I will."

"Have you looked at the sky?"

Yes.

He had.

"Pretty cool, huh?" Poon said. "That's really going to increase the intensity. With any luck, that plane will be rocking like a leaf in a hurricane."

Kong grunted.

"Yeah, we can only hope."

Kong got to the airport a half hour early and paced as he waited for the pilot. The sky didn't improve. If anything, it got worse.

Poon.

How did he get so twisted?

One thing was sure, it didn't happen overnight.

If Kong understood what was going on—and he was pretty sure he did—Poon had a yearly bet going with six or seven or eight other people. The bet was to see which one of them could scare a person the most and capture that terror on film. The winner got a million Hong Kong dollars, which wasn't a lot, but was enough to make things more interesting than just the bragging rights.

Poon's plan this year was simple, brilliantly simple,

sickly simple.

Poon would hire the 22-year-old bombshell who was unconscious on his bed—Fion. He'd hire her for the day and pay her in advance, a good deal of money, and tell her to just stay at home until he called with instructions and told her what he wanted her to do.

She'd say fine.

She'd stay home.

She'd wait for instructions.

Poon would call her and tell her to take a cab to the airport, Gate 7.

She'd do it.

Kong would be waiting for her, introduce himself as a pilot, and tell her that Poon wanted her to go on a little flight. She'd say fine. Kong would direct her to the aisle seat in the third row. He would secure her to the seat with duct tap around her wrists, torso and legs. Then he'd blindfold her.

She wouldn't protest.

The pilot would then sneak quietly on board. Kong would stay in the cockpit and pretend he was the one flying. Once they got to altitude, the pilot would put the plane on autopilot and hide behind a seat in the back of the plane.

Kong would then take the woman's blindfold off.

Then he'd put a parachute on.

"What are you going?" she'd ask.

Kong would just shake his head disapprovingly and said, "I don't know what you did to Poon to make him want you to die this way, but it sure must have been something."

Then he'd jump out of the plane.

The woman would go hysterical.

That hysteria would be beautifully captured by a small but high quality camera that would transmit the scene to Poon where it would be recorded.

After five minutes or so, the pilot would step out of hiding, take the controls and tell her it was all just a joke.

They'd land safely.

No one would get hurt.

Fion would forgive Poon because he paid her so well.

The pilot showed up at ten sharp and asked, "Are you the actor?"

"That's me."

"Got a little chop up there today," the man said. "Be careful when you jump. Don't open your chute until you have to. That way there'll be less time for things to go wrong. I'm glad that you're doing that part and not me."

Fion showed up at 11:00, right on schedule.

Fifteen minutes later, the plane lifted off the runway and climbed into a swirling charcoal sky.

18

August 7
Friday Morning

Prarie pitched and turned all night, waiting for Emmanuelle to return to the hotel. But she didn't. Not at three in the morning, or four, or five.

Dawn broke.

Prarie wasn't in the mood for it, not even close, and stayed under the covers. She was sound asleep when she detected movement and heard the shower running.

"Is that you?" she shouted.

No answer.

Two minutes later, the water shut off.

"Is that you?"

"Yeah."

"Where were you all night?"

"Hunting."

Emmanuelle emerged from the bathroom naked, crawled under the covers and said, "I need sleep like you can't even believe."

"Have you been up all night?"

"Every freaking minute of it," Emmanuelle said. "Be a princess and rub my back, will you?"

Prarie did.

"You scared me half to death."

Emmanuelle didn't respond.

She was already asleep.

She didn't move until noon. Then she rolled onto her back, stretched and said, "Coffee, I need coffee—food too, coffee and food."

"What happened last night?"

Emmanuelle grunted.

"I made a move on the rock star."

"And?"

"And I need coffee."

19

August 7
Friday Morning

Friday morning, Teffinger woke up in a strange room next to a naked woman—Fan Rae Fan—just as dawn broke over Hong Kong. He studied the sensuous curves of her body for a second and felt sorry for every guy in the world who wasn't him. Outside, the life-sounds of the city were already resonating.

He felt good.

He dressed without waking Fan Rae, gave her an imperceptible kiss on the cheek, closed the door gently on his way out and took a cab to the Fleming.

Then he went for a three-mile jog.

Clouds filled the sky.

There would be rain today, lots of rain.

He could already tell.

He showered and just got toweled off when his phone rang and the voice of Sydney Heatherwood came through. "I got the surveillance tapes from that bar," she said. "It was raining heavy and the lighting was bad."

Teffinger exhaled.

"Good," he said.

Silence.

"Well, not that good," Sydney said. "Things were clear enough to show a white pickup truck. And there's a second, more like half a second, where your face shows in the window. You actually turned and looked towards the building."

Teffinger remembered the moment.

"And?" he said.

"And to me it looked like you," Sydney said. "Don't panic, though. I think that the only reason it looked like you is because I already knew it was you. If I had been seeing it for the first time and didn't know it was you, I don't think you would even enter my head. I would just be thinking it was some white guy, and that would be about it."

"What about the license plate?"

"It never showed."

Okay.

Good.

"Be sure the tape gets in the file," he said.

"It already is. How are things going over there?"

"I met a woman," he said.

"Who?"

"The detective, Fan Rae Fan."

"And?"

"And I could be happy with her."

"What does that mean, exactly?"

"I'm not sure."

Silence.

Then Sydney said, "You're not thinking of moving there, are you?"

"I don't know what I'm thinking," he said. "To be honest, d'Asia hasn't quite left my thoughts."

"Teffinger, you need to slow down," she said. "You always move too fast. You know that."

True.

He did.

"I don't exactly plan this stuff. It's more like getting hit in the face with a rock. There it is, deal with it."

"Two rocks."

Teffinger chuckled and said, "Yeah, two rocks. I'll keep you posted. By the way, I told her what I did—her, meaning Fan Rae. She's going to help me find d'Asia."

"Unbelievable."

He almost hung up and then said, "Hey, you still there?"

"Yes."

"I almost forgot to say thanks."

"Okay, you're welcome. For what?"

"For not getting dirty," he said. "If you had done that, I don't know how I could have lived with myself."

He hung up and got dressed.

Two minutes later, Fan Rae called.

"Where are you?"

"The hotel."

"Someone saw our beach victim on the news last night and thinks she might be a woman who lives in his apartment building, someone named Nuwa Moon. I'm going to head over and check it out. You want to tag along?"

He did, he did indeed.

"Be out front in ten minutes."

They headed to the other side of the city, west of Central, to an area where cheap-but-good eateries and grocery stores and Laundromats sat at street level with six or eight floors of apartments stacked up top, typical city living.

"When did you leave?" Fan Rea asked.

"Just a little bit ago," Teffinger said. "Dawn or thereabouts."

"I thought maybe you left in the middle of the night."

No.

He didn't.

"I needed a jog and a shower and clothes that didn't smell like smoke," he said. "I didn't want to wake you."

"Next time wake me."

"Okay."

"You promise?"

"You looked so peaceful."

"Screw peaceful," she said. "Next time wake me."

According to the caller, Nuwa Moon lived in apartment 308. Fan Rae bypassed the elevators, headed for the stairwell and said, "I usually walk. I like the exercise."

Teffinger shrugged and said, "Fine with me."

They knocked on the door.

No response came.

The doorknob didn't turn.

"We'll need to find the manager," Fan Rae said.

Ten minutes later they were inside.

Inside a small cubical with a sofa-bed and a bathroom, to be precise. "I couldn't live here in a million years," Teffinger said.

"This is typical Hong Kong."

"Two million, even."

A photograph on the refrigerator showed that Nuwa Moon was in fact the dead woman with the carving on her stomach. There was another woman in the picture, too—a young woman, equally g-punk, with her arm around Nuwa's shoulders and a cynical smirk on her lips.

Pretty.

"It looks like our victim had a friend," Fan Rae said. "I'll bet if we talk to her, she'll know something."

Teffinger agreed, but that's not where his thoughts were.

He walked over to the only window, pulled the curtain shut and found it was thick enough to bring the room into a deep darkness. Then he picked Fan Rae up, carried her to the couch and laid her down on her back.

"Here?" she said.
"I can't wait another minute."
Then he took her.
Hard.
Like an animal.

20

August 7
Friday Morning

Fion seemed like a nice girl. Kong had no desire to scare her to death, but a job was a job. The pilot climbed to ten thousand feet, put on the autopilot and started the digital camera transmission. Then he whispered in Kong's ear—"Jump in exactly three minutes"—and hid in the back. Kong took the blindfold off Fion, got into character and slipped the parachute on as she watched.

"I don't know what you did to deserve this," he said. "But look at it this way—we all have to die at some point. You're luckier than most, actually, because it'll be so fast that you won't even feel it."

The plane pitched and tossed.

Violently.

Loudly.

To the front and above, the sky was clear.

The clouds were below.

Black.

Twirling.

Laced with lightning.

Kong couldn't see the ground. It would be insanity to jump, but the game had gone too far to back out.

The woman screamed and pleaded and pulled at her bonds, louder than Kong thought.

He ignored her as best he could.

His thoughts were on what he was about to do.

A violent downdraft suddenly grabbed the plane and dropped it for one, two, three, four, five seconds. Then it slammed into a floor of air. If Kong had jumped just then, the wing would have cracked his skull.

He checked his watch.

Ten seconds.

Nine.

Eight.

He muscled the door open.

The force of the wind was incredible.

It was all he could do to get his body wedged in.

"See you in hell!" he said.

The woman screamed.

Kong listened for a second.

Then he jumped.

21

August 7
Friday Noon

Emmanuelle told Prarie the story as they drank coffee and walked outside at the harbour's edge. The sky was mean and complicated. The story by contrast was short and simple. Emmanuelle made a move on the rock star after Prarie left last night. He wasn't rude but was interested, either, and ended up leaving an hour later with curvy black-haired beauty in a tight red dress. Emmanuelle followed them to an apartment six blocks away, which she surmised belonged to the woman because she pulled keys out of a purse just before they entered.

Emmanuelle hung in the shadows across the street, waiting for the rock star to emerge.

He didn't.

Not for an hour.

Or another.

Or another.

Then he did, shortly before dawn.

She followed him to the Causeway Bay Typhoon Shelter. There he fired up a dinghy at a wooden dock and disappeared into the darkness. "Obviously one of the boats moored out there is his, but I have no idea which one," Emmanuelle said.

"So now what?"

A seagull swooped out of the sky, grabbed a chunk of bread off the sidewalk, and took off.

Two other gulls gave chase, trying to steal the food in mid-flight.

"At this point, I think we need to buy a pair of good binoculars," Emmanuelle said. "It shouldn't be too hard to find him from shore if we're patient enough. The main thing is for you to get a better look at him so we can figure out if he's the right guy or not."

"I'd be clearer if I could hear his voice," Prarie said.

"Understood, but that might not be so easy," Emmanuelle said. "We need to be careful. If he sees me, he'll know something's up. And we definitely can't let him see you." Prarie must have had a look on her face because Emmanuelle said, "How are you holding up? Are you okay?"

Prarie nodded.

"I've sort of given up hope on finishing out the semester," she said.

"Sorry."

"My head's so far out of the books at this point that it isn't even funny. It looks like I'm yours until this thing is resolved."

Emmanuelle pulled out her cell phone and called the art galley guy, the one who had her $1,000 HKD in his wallet. "It's me," she said. "You were going to make some calls regarding a replica painting."

"Yes, I've been waiting for you," he said. "Do you have a pencil handy?"

She did, and wrote down a name—Danny Wing Wan—and a number.

"Do you want some advice?" the man asked.

"Sure."

"Forget the painting," he said. "Most of these replica guys are involved with fraud to one degree or another. Sometimes they're not nice people, if you catch my drift."

"Consider the drift caught. Thanks."

She hung up, looked at Prarie and said, "Got a name and number, but it comes with a warning."

The wind blew Prarie's hair over her face.

She pulled it to the side and held it.

"So what do we do?"

"We keep moving forward," Emmanuelle said. "Things are going to get dicey from this point on. When we pick up the binoculars, we'll get a couple of survival knives too."

"You're kidding, right?"

No, she wasn't.

22

August 7
Friday Morning

Inside the apartment of the victim, Nuwa Moon, they found a pile of newspaper clippings about young women who had disappeared. "I wonder if one of these missing girls was a friend of hers," Teffinger said.

Fan Rae titled her head.

"More to the point, she must think they're all connected somehow. Why? What does she know that we don't?"

Teffinger shrugged.

"I don't know, but she probably talked about it to this woman right here," he said, tapping the photograph on the fridge.

After five more minutes of looking around, they figured out the friend's name.

It was *Syling Wu.*

Syling Wu lived at Flat 301, 3F, No. 137, Sai Wan

Ho Street, Sai Wan Ho, six kilometers east of Central. The street was typical Hong Kong, with street-level shops and housing above, accessed by a single door and a flight of stairs. Several scooters sat on the street to the right. Many of the shops had sun-bleached canvas canopies. Signs cantilevered out from the buildings, but they weren't as large or as many as on the streets to the west. The buildings weren't as high, either—most topped out at four stories.

The sky was dark and twisty.

"It's going to storm like the devil today," Fan Rae said.

Teffinger looked up but then spotted something more important.

"Would they sell coffee over there?" he asked, pointing.

"Yes."

Beautiful.

Beyond beautiful.

Five minutes later, with coffee in hand, they climbed three flights of stairs and knocked on the woman's door.

No one answered.

Teffinger tried the knob.

It didn't turn.

He frowned and said, "Now what?"

Fan Rae stood there for a second sipping coffee, then turned and knocked on the door across the hall-way. The door opened timidly for a few inches before a chain snagged it. The face of a young woman appeared. She was holding a baby.

Fan Rae talked to her in Cantonese for a couple of minutes.

Then the door shut and she said, "She doesn't know where Syling is and doesn't know much about her, other than she works as a hostess girl at a placed called the High Tide Bar."

A hostess girl?

"What's a hostess girl?"

"You don't know what a hostess girl is?"

No.

He didn't.

"You'll find out tonight, if she doesn't show up beforehand."

Teffinger almost pressed the issue but his thoughts had gone elsewhere—to d'Asia. He came here to help her and hadn't done a thing.

He needed to get refocused, right now, this minute.

Then something popped into his head.

"Have you ever heard of someone called Billy Shek?"

"Billy Shek?"

"Right."

She paused, processing it, then looked at him and said, "No. It's not ringing a bell."

"He's a photographer."

She shrugged.

"Don't know him. Why?"

"D'Asia knows him," Teffinger said. "He's the

one who told her to come and see me."

"If you want, we can head back to the office and run him down," she said.

He wanted.

"No problem," Fan Rae said. "I want to get back there anyway and pull the files on all these missing women. I'm really anxious to see if they're connected somehow."

23

August 7
Friday Morning

Kong plunged towards earth. The wind was more dangerous than he thought. It created a wicked vacuum that hardly let him breathe. Then things got worse—he entered the clouds.

Arcs of lightning exploded around him, deafening, deadly.

He tried to see the ground to gauge his height but saw nothing. His fingers held the ripcord with an iron grip.

Pull now?

Wait?

Five seconds, wait five more seconds.

He waited three seconds and pulled. The chute opened and snagged him. Then it collapsed, and he dropped, almost as fast as before but not quite.

His heart raced.

He was going to die.

He should have known better.

He should have never jumped.

The chute's drag slowed him to some extent, but he released it before he got tangled. He dropped faster. Then suddenly he saw the ground, closer than it should have been.

He was too low, way too low.

He pulled the cord for the emergency chute as fast as he could.

It snagged him and fluttered, about to collapse.

Second after second passed.

Then he hit the ground hard, three times more forceful than he should have. He tucked and rolled.

He didn't die.

He immediately got to his feet, desperate to see if his body still functioned.

He walked, forwards, sideways, backwards, testing his legs, waving his arms, rolling his neck.

Everything hurt but nothing was broken.

Then something bad happened.

In the distance, the plane pierced through the bottom of the clouds, nose first, spinning out of control and heading straight down at an amazing speed.

Pull up!

Pull up!

But the pull didn't come, not at all, not even at the last second.

Then an explosion came. A bright orange fireball rolled upwards into the sky followed by the thickest, blackest smoke Kong had ever seen.

He wrestled out of the chute, dropped it to the

dirt and ran in the other direction.

The implications were already upon him. His life had changed, just like that, because Fion and the pilot were dead. If Jack Poon got tied to it, he might be criminally liable.

Kong was one person who could tie him to the event, meaning that Poon might be better off if Kong was dead.

Would Poon kill him?

24

August 7
Friday Morning

Kong hadn't been on the ground for more than ten minutes when Jack Poon called and said, "We need to talk." An hour later Kong walked into Poon's penthouse, apprehensive. "You're probably wondering what happened," Poon said. "Let me show you."

A flat-panel TV turned on.

Kong watched.

He saw himself jump out of the plane. He watched Fion go absolutely crazy with fear. When the pilot finally emerged from hiding and started to make his way to the cockpit, a terrible downdraft rolled the plane and sent it spiraling. The pilot fought to get to the controls but never made it. Then the transmission stopped.

"It's not my fault and it's not your fault," Poon said. "The pilot is the one who had the responsibility to stay out of the sky if the plane couldn't handle it. I didn't hold a gun to his head and neither did you. We could have done it tomorrow just as easily."

Kong nodded.

That was true to some extent.

"You did your part and you did it good," Poon said. He handed Kong an envelope and added, "So good that I'm kicking in a little bonus."

Kong took it and opened it briefly, just long enough to see it was a lot of money.

He shoved it in his back pocket.

"Thanks," he said.

"Even though what happened isn't your fault or mine, it would probably be a good idea to never tell anyone what happened."

"Exactly."

"Good," Poon said. "We're in agreement. Of course, using the transmission is now out of the question. One of the rules is that the person being scared can't actually die or be harmed. So I have to think of something new. My question to you is whether you want to be a part of it, once I get it figured out."

Kong shrugged.

"Sure, why not?" He grinned and added, "As long as there aren't any parachutes involved."

Poon grinned and slapped Kong on the back.

25

August 7
Friday Afternoon

The wind got meaner and then the rain came. Prarie and Emmanuelle bought a good pair of binoculars and two eight-inch, light-weight, razor-sharp survival knives, which went into their purses. Then they hugged the east shore of the Causeway Bay Typhoon Shelter and surveyed the boats—hundreds of which were moored in an eclectic seascape of old meets new, east meets west. Many of the vessels were modern, expensive yachts. Just as many were old, Chinese junks, throwbacks to an age all but gone, with live-aboard families.

A sizeable break-wall ran along the north edge of the shelter, giving it protection from Victoria Harbour.

Breakers bashed against it.

Even inside the wall, the water was anything but calm.

Choppy whitecaps bobbed the boats and stretched

their mooring ropes.

Prarie trained the binoculars on the vessels for all of two minutes and said, "Forget it, no one's out. Everyone's taking shelter from the weather."

They headed for the Metro, soaked.

Before they got there, something weird happened.

The storm blew past just like that.

They sky got calm.

The sun peeked through the haze.

They headed back to the water.

Fifteen minutes later, they spotted the rock star on a fairly large sailboat that had Dangerous Lady written in English on the side. He got into a dinghy with the same name, pulled the rope of a small outboard motor, untied a line at the stern and headed west, towards the Royal Hong Kong Yacht Club.

"Come on, hurry," Emmanuelle said.

The rock star was just leaving the area when they got there, nicely dressed and carrying a briefcase.

"He's going somewhere," Emmanuelle said.

"I see that."

"What I mean is, a meeting or something. He's not going to be back for a while. This is our chance."

"To do what?"

"To go aboard, what do you think?"

"Why? What's onboard?"

Emmanuelle shrugged.

"I'll know it when I see it," she said. "Here's the plan. I'm going alone. I'm going to use his dinghy, because that's what's supposed to be tied to his boat.

You're going to stay on shore and call me if he shows up."

"And what if he does?"

"I don't know," Emmanuelle said. "Hopefully he won't."

"Be careful."

"I will."

"You can swim, right?"

Emmanuelle hesitated.

"Not exactly."

"You can't swim?"

"No."

"Not even a little?"

"No."

"Well if you fall in, you're dead."

"I won't fall in."

Prarie exhaled, wondering if she was going to actually say what she was about to say, and then said it—"I'll go, you stay here."

"I'll be fine."

"I'm not going to argue about it."

Emmanuelle looked as if she was about to reply, but then she said, "The hatch might be locked. If it is, pry it open with your knife. If you find a laptop, grab it."

They took one last look around to be sure the rock star was gone, then walked down to the dinghy, which was tied at a wooden dock, dinghy city. People were around, but no one paid attention. Prarie got in as if she owned it, fired up the outboard and pointed the bow towards Dangerous Lady.

An old woman on a colorful junk hung clothes and gave Prarie a long stare as she motored past.

Prarie waved.

The woman waved back and then disappeared inside.

Two minutes later, Prarie reached Dangerous Lady and tied up.

The door to the cabin was closed but not locked. Good.

She walked down six steps and looked around.

Ample light came through the portals.

The floor was teak.

The sink was full of dishes.

The bed was unmade.

Stuff was everywhere.

A flat-screen TV was off.

Then something caught her eye; a semi-automatic pistol, black.

She never held a gun before and found it heavier than she expected. Then she looked around for a safety, found it, and figured out how to flick it off.

What are you for?

To get drunk and shoot seagulls?

Suddenly her cell phone rang and a panic-laced voice came through—"He's back!"

"You got to be kidding—"

"He's standing right where his dinghy was, looking around for it."

"Damn it."

"You got to get out of there."

"I just got on board. I haven't even looked around yet," Prarie said.

"There's no time. Get in the dinghy and head east. I'll meet you over there."

"No."

"But—"

"Just stay where you are and keep an eye on him," Prarie said. "If he actually gets in something and starts heading this way, let me know."

"That'll be too late. You'll be trapped."

"We're wasting time," Prarie said.

Then she hung up and looked around with the gun in hand.

Talk to me, Dangerous Lady.

Talk to me fast.

26

August 7
Friday Afternoon

Teffinger shored up on coffee and watched while Fan Rae worked the computer, looking for Billy Shek and having lots of luck—all of it bad. There were a billion Sheks in the city, but no Billy. "Lots of people go by a western name but never officially change their legal name," Fan Ray said. "It's a real problem."

"So I see."

It was another dead end.

Wait, maybe not.

"Can you cross-reference the Sheks to photographers?" he asked.

She shook her head.

"No."

Okay.

Dead end.

The computer wasn't any kinder when they searched for Syling Wu. It was as if she didn't exist.

Weird.

"You know what I need?" he asked.

No.

She didn't.

"A thermos."

"A thermos? Why?"

"For coffee," he said. "I like to have it with me."

His cell phone rang. It was Sydney so he stepped into the hall and answered. "How are things going over there?" she asked.

Teffinger grunted.

"I've never spent so much time going absolutely nowhere," he said. "I'm not a single inch closer to finding d'Asia than I was two years ago before I even met her."

"Yeah, well, that doesn't make two of us."

"Meaning what?"

"Meaning I've had a few developments," she said. "Double-F bumped into me and asked how things were going on that railroad case. I told him about the videotape. He said to give it to Kwak and see if he could enhance it."

Teffinger twisted a pencil in his fingers, then snapped it in half.

"Do it," he said.

"I will, obviously, but that's not the main reason I called," Sydney said. "One of the black-and-whites picked up a homeless guy for trespassing down at the tracks this morning. They got to talking. The guy said he was there the night the woman got dumped.

He was sleeping in a boxcar when headlights woke him up. He looked outside and saw a pickup truck. A white man pulled a woman from the bed of the truck and dumped her on the ground. He got a good luck at the guy."

"How could he?"

"He said the guy dumped her near the front of the truck and the headlights lit his face up pretty good."

Teffinger remembered it.

He paced.

"I took his statement and then he spent an hour working with a sketch artist, but without any luck," she added. "So there won't be a composite sketch going on the news tonight. This guy swears though that he'll recognize the guy if he ever sees him again."

She paused, waiting.

"What's his name?" Teffinger asked.

"Charles DeFry."

"Don't know him," he said. "Maybe he'll wander off to some other town."

"He's been in Denver for five years."

"Of course he has."

"Even the winters," she added.

Fan Rae appeared with a brisk step and grabbed Teffinger's arm as she walked past.

"Come on."

"Where we going?"

"To a bar I just found out about from an anonymous caller," she said.

"Why? What's there?"

"Smoke, if my hunch is right," she said. "The same smoke that was in Nuwa Moon's hair."

"Wait a minute."

He disappeared down the hall, into the kitchenette, and reappeared ten seconds later with a cup of coffee in hand.

"Okay," he said.

Hong Kong starts at sea level but quickly rises as it stretches south out of Victoria Harbour. Within a short distance, the terrain gets too steep to build skyscrapers and the cityscape screeches to a stop. From the air, the city looks like a long thin strip of congestion sandwiched between the water and the mountains. The higher portion of the city is called the Mid-Levels. An enclosed escalator runs for several blocks and connects the sea level portion of the city to the Mid-Levels. In the morning, the escalator only runs downward. After ten, it runs both ways.

That's what Teffinger and Fan Rae ended up taking, the escalator, which carved through SoHo.

They got off on Conduit Road and walked west for three blocks, staying on the shady side of the street. Then they came to a bar called Hei Yewan, which turned out to be a large underground hideaway, barely noticeable from the outside.

It was closed but when they pounded on the door, someone finally answered—a man about 25, dressed in all things black, heavily pierced and tattooed. His hair was spiked and dyed pink.

Fan Rae explained who she was and asked,

"What's your name?"

"Dustin."

"No, your real name."

"On Yu Liou."

"Are you the owner?"

"No, I'm the manager."

"Show me the back room," she said. The man hesitated and Fan Rae said, "Just do it. I'm not in the mood."

They walked through a large dark space big enough to hold three hundred drunks, with a cement floor, black walls, multiple bar areas and dozens of speakers. At the back was a velvet rope guarding a black door.

Teffinger pictured a doorman there at night.

Dustin unlocked it.

They walked down a short black hallway.

He unlocked a second door.

Beyond that was a room, a large one. On the cement floor, in red spray paint, was a K'ung chia symbol.

"Tell me about this room," Fan Rae said.

27

August 7
Friday Afternoon

Get out of there now! He just jumped in another dinghy and he's heading your way!"

As soon as she heard the words, Prarie slammed the phone in her pocket, grabbed the only thing she had found of interest—a laptop—and ran up the stairs.

Then she had a second thought, bounded down below and grabbed the gun.

She was in the dinghy and had it untied in a heartbeat. It drifted while she pulled the rope for the outboard. It sputtered but wouldn't catch. She pulled again, and again, frantic.

It choked and spit blue smoke, refusing to start.

Damn it!

It was flooded.

She twisted the gas to full throttle and pulled again. It sputtered twice and then fired. She jammed it in gear and headed east at full throttle. The bow slammed into the waves and threw cold salt spray in her face.

She turned and checked behind her.

What she saw she could hardly believe.

The rock star was closing fast, shouting and waving a fist.

There was no way she'd get to shore before he reached her.

Shit!

What to do?

Up ahead was a bridge for a major road, held up by massive piers rising out of the harbour. She jammed the gun in her belt, swung around the closest one and dived over the side as soon as she got out of sight.

The dinghy went south; faster now, without her weight.

The sound of the other engine got louder.

She ducked under the surface just before it got around the pier. When she surfaced, the rock star was in hot pursuit of the runaway—so beautiful.

Then something bad happened.

He carved to the left and doubled back.

She stayed under the water as much as she could, rising only to take a quick gulp of air.

Minute after minute passed.

The man didn't leave.

He was trolling and circling, waiting for her to get so tired that she'd have to break the surface and flail her arms. It was only a matter of time before he spotted her. Then the worst possible thing happened, he came directly at her, on a collision course. She got as far under the surface as she could, frantic about the propeller. Then as he passed overhead, she pulled the gun and got ready.

Suddenly the engine revved.

The dinghy sped away.

She stayed under as long as she could.

When she rose, she saw him speeding to the other dinghy, which had lodged against the south shore. Then she saw why.

Emmanuelle was there, spotting the laptop, grabbing it and running like crazy.

28

August 7
Friday Afternoon

The back room of Hei Yewan got used for a private affair on Wednesday, the night Nuwa Moon ended up with a K'ung chia symbol carved in her 22-year-old stomach.

"Used by who?" Fan Rae asked.

Dustin, the manager, scratched a tattoo and shrugged.

"I don't know."

"Bullshit."

"Honest," he said. "Everyone came and went by the back door. The two doors that we just went through, they were locked the whole time."

"So who knows who was here?"

"I don't know," he said. "Not me, though. I don't have anything to do with this part of the place. I only manage the front and that's where I was."

They pressed for information and got none.

He denied knowing if the room was used for

pagan purposes. He also denied ever seeing Nuwa Moon or Syling Wu, either on Wednesday or on any other day.

They escorted the man out of the room and shut the door.

"He's lying about not knowing Nuwa Moon," Fan Rae said. "This is the exact kind of place she would hang out and she's way to pretty to miss. Dustin's a horn dog. He was even checking me out." A pause then, "I don't see any blood on the floor, at least to my naked eye. We'll give forensics a call, though, and let them shine the lights. Public records will tell us who the owner is. It'll be a corporation because everything here is. But we should be able to peel that back and squeeze the principals."

Teffinger understood.

They had a liquor license they wouldn't want to lose.

Answers were out there, they would just take time and effort.

"We should stop in here tonight, have a drink and show Nuwa Moon's picture around," Teffinger said. "Do you think they play any Beach Boys songs?"

Someone knocked on the door and then pushed it open, tentatively. Teffinger expected Dustin, but it turned out to be a woman with black glasses, attractive, almost on par with Fan Rae, wearing white shorts and an eggshell-blue tank top over a very nice non-pierced, non-tattooed, non-g-punk body. She was taller than most, about thirty, and wore her hair short and stylish.

She had a classy, exotic look.

She could be a model or a corporate executive.

As interesting as she was, Teffinger's focus shifted to Fan Rae, who seemed to be in shock.

"We need to talk," the woman said to Fan Rae. The words were in English. A glance at him meant, "In private."

"Hey, no problem," he said.

He headed down the hall, then to the restroom.

When he got back to the hallway, the women were still talking—no, not talking, whispering. He hung there, trying to figure out if they were done enough for him to go back in. He could only pick up bits and pieces of the conversation, but definitely heard the word d'Asia, several times in fact.

Weird.

He tiptoed closer.

Then heard a clear sentence from the lips of the mystery woman, "I'm going to kill her, end of story. You can help or not, your choice. Either way she's dead."

Silence.

"When?" Fan Rae asked.

"Soon."

"Call me before you do anything," Fan Rae said.

"Does that mean you're going to help?"

A pause.

Then Fan Rae said, "I don't know. I got to think it through." Then she lowered her voice and said, "Don't say anything to that guy in the other room.

He came here to protect her."

"Who is he?"

"A detective from the United States. I'll fill you in later."

The talking stopped and Teffinger backed out of the hallway. Thirty seconds later, the mystery woman walked into the main bar at a brisk pace and threw him a sideways glance before she pushed through the front door.

Teffinger headed to the symbol room.

"Who was that?" he asked.

Fan Rae shook her head as if it was no biggie.

"Just someone from work."

"Oh."

"I'm going to call forensics," she said, referring to the hunt for bloodstains.

Fine.

Good idea.

"I'm going to head out and find some coffee," he said.

"You are so addicted."

He was already in the hallway, walking fast.

"You want some?"

"No."

Outside, he looked for the mystery woman.

She wasn't to the left, or the right, or across the street.

Damn it!

She was nowhere.

He headed to the right at a trot, which turned out

to be a good move.

There she was up ahead, weaving quickly through the crowd.

He hung back thirty paces and followed.

His heart was heavy.

Fan Ran wasn't who he thought she was.

He was alone.

The city felt cold.

29

August 7
Friday Afternoon

The woman on shore ran with the spirit of a deer being chased by sharp yellow teeth. She escaped but Kong got a good enough look at her to tell she was the same woman who hit on him at D-Drop last night. As for the other woman, the one in the dinghy, she disappeared after rounding the pier and Kong never got a good look at her.

Maybe she escaped.

Maybe she drowned.

Hopefully the latter.

Back at Dangerous Lady, everything seemed intact except for the laptop and the gun. He didn't care about the gun and in fact was glad it was gone. It was illegal as hell and could only bring trouble.

Good riddance.

The laptop was a different story.

He needed to get it back.

The best he could figure, the woman in the dinghy was the person blackmailing him. She must have recruited the other woman, who tried to pick him up last night, with intents of having him take her back to his place where she could snoop around in hopes of getting even more dirt. When that didn't work, they decided to break in.

Well, screw that.

That insanity was going to end.

It was time.

He called Kam Lee Yao and said, "Where are you?"

"At the establishment."

Kong chuckled.

"I'm going to come over and talk to you."

"Why, what's going on?"

"I'll tell you when I get there."

Kam Lee owned and operated the best dungeon in Hong Kong. It sat in the hills south of the city, on Bowen Road not far from Lover's Rock. Outside, it looked like a mansion. Inside, it was a world unlike all others—a world of addictions, a world of secrets, a world of forbidden pleasures. Kam Lee didn't know it at the time, but her kinky side took hold at age ten, when a pack of boys held her down spread-eagle on the ground and took turns tickling her to death.

That incident laid dormant for ten years.

Then she began to explore.

She preferred to be a top.

In fact, she was always a top.

Well, not always.

She'd submit to a certain few.

Kong was one of those few.

She had a stable of lovelies, available 24/7, tops and bottoms, varied enough to satisfy even the most extreme desires. They were pricey, make no mistake about that, but they were worth every penny. There were ten soundproof rooms with a variety of themes; dark dungeons, bedrooms, devices. Five women were on hand at all times to handle the walk-ins—fifteen on the weekends.

The girls' schedules were posted on the website.

Clients could pay cash or credit.

Confidentiality was paramount.

Special arrangements were available for high-profile clients or anyone else who wanted absolute discretion. They would be picked up by car, driven to the back door, and escorted in total secrecy to one of the rooms. If they wanted, the slave could even be blindfolded the entire time and never even know who the session was with.

When Kong showed up, Fan Lee ran a finger down his chest and said, "So what's going on?"

He looked around and said, "Let's talk in private."

She took him into a room that had a number of devices—a cross, a rack, and an assortment of sexual furniture—and closed the door.

He exhaled.

"I need your help with something."

"How bad do you need it?"

"Bad," he said.

She smiled and said, "Good."

Then she slid her dress off her shoulders and let it drop to the floor. She wore nothing underneath, other than a drop-dead gorgeous body.

"Do a session with me and I'll help you," she said.

"You don't even know what I want you to do yet."

"It doesn't matter."

Kong cocked his head.

"It might be dangerous."

"Repeat, it doesn't matter."

"Now?"

She nodded.

"You're the only one I trust enough," she said. "I've been in the mood for a month."

Then she laid on her back on the rack and stretched her arms over her head. Kong knew what to do, he'd done it before. He stretched her out, tight, so that she was barely able to move.

"Comfy?" he asked.

"Yes."

"How long of a session to you want?"

"A half hour."

The words shocked him.

The longest session to this point had been ten minutes.

"Really?"

"Yes," she said, "and no matter what I do or say, don't stop. I want the full half hour. Promise me."

"If that's what you want."

"That's what I want."

30

August 7
Friday Afternoon

Prarie made it to shore without drowning or getting killed by the rock star but couldn't find Emmanuelle, so she headed back to the Inter-Continental.

Good thing, too.

Emmanuelle was there.

They hugged.

"That was too close," Emmanuelle said.

True, very true.

"The laptop got a lot of water on it but it still turns on," Emmanuelle added. "Unfortunately it has a security password so I haven't been able to get in yet. Once we do get in, I have no idea whether everything will be in English or Cantonese."

Prarie frowned.

Neither of them spoke Cantonese, much less read it.

Her hair was dry but felt like straw. She ran her

fingers through it, headed for the shower and said, "I need to wash this salt off."

"Go for it. Hey, it's nice to have you still alive."

"Likewise."

When Prarie got out, Emmanuelle was pacing.

Something was wrong.

"I called that number the gallery guy gave us," Emmanuelle said. "The thousand dollar number."

"You mean the replica guy?"

"Right. He's willing to meet."

"Good."

"He sounded weird," Emmanuelle said.

"Then forget him."

"We don't have that luxury. We're just going to need to be careful."

"When does he want to do it?"

"Tonight. Are you tired? Do you want to take a nap or anything?"

Prarie shook her head.

"I'm too wound up," she said. "But I need food in the worst way."

"Okay, but no swimming for thirty minutes."

Prarie rolled her eyes.

"Not funny," she said.

"A little funny."

"Okay, maybe a little."

They walked up Nathan Street and ended up in a noisy noodle place with wooden floors and sturdy tables and throngs of people jamming food into their mouths as if they were on ten-minute timers.

They ordered.

Their food showed up in two minutes, tasty and cheap.

Prarie told Emmanuelle how she stayed under the water to avoid getting caught. "I was half ready to shoot him when your little episode over on the shore got him distracted. In a way, you saved my life."

Emmanuelle stared at her.

"Shoot him with what?"

"The gun—didn't I tell you about that?"

No.

She didn't.

So she did.

"What did you do with it?"

"The gun?"

"Right."

"I just left it there on the shore," she said. "Why?"

"Do you think it's still there?"

Prarie shrugged.

"I don't know. Probably—"

"Let's go get it."

Prarie shook her head. "Guns are illegal in Hong Kong," she said. "If you get caught with one, you're going to jail, period, end of sentence. And the jails here aren't nice."

Emmanuelle chewed noodles and considered it.

Then she said, "I'd rather have it than not, at least tonight. If things go okay with the replica guy, we'll dump it afterwards."

Prarie shook her head.

"We got the knives," she said.

Yes, they did.

"Knives aren't guns," Emmanuelle said.

Prarie studied the woman.

"This guy really has you spooked," she said.

"No, I'm just being cautious."

Prarie rolled her eyes.

"Spooked with a capital S."

Emmanuelle smiled.

"Okay, spooked, but not with a capital."

They paid the bill and then took the MRT to the Causeway Bay Typhoon Shelter. The rock star was nowhere to be seen but the gun was, right where Prarie left it. Emmanuelle brushed the dirt off and stuck it in her purse.

"Do you think it will still fire?" Prarie asked.

Emmanuelle nodded.

"It should, so long as the water didn't get to the gunpowder."

"How do we know if that happened or not?"

Emmanuelle looked around, saw no one close, stuck the tip of the barrel in the water and pulled the trigger. Water splashed into her face. She wiped it off with the back of her hand and said, "There's our answer. We should clean it though so the salt doesn't jam it up."

Prarie tilted her head, impressed.

"You're such an organized little criminal."

"Criminal hunter," Emmanuelle said. "There's a difference."

31

August 7
Friday Afternoon

The mystery woman walked east towards Central for five minutes and then hopped on a double-decker bus just as it took off. Teffinger looked for a cab, spotted one ten steps ahead and pounded on the passenger-side glass. Two people in the back recoiled to the opposite side. The driver shouted something and waved a fist.

Shit!

Then he ran after the bus, weaving through bodies and trying to not knock anyone over.

People stared.

He didn't care.

They weren't the problem. The problem was the heat and the humidity. The bus came to a stop a half block ahead.

People got on.

People got off, but not the mystery woman.

It pulled away when Teffinger was twenty steps

behind it.

Damn it!

How far to the next stop?

Two blocks?

Three?

He kept going.

He had to.

This was the person who was out to kill d'Asia.

This was Teffinger's chance, maybe his only chance.

He fought through the sweat and the pain and kept going.

At the next stop, the woman didn't get off, and the bus pulled away just before he got to it.

One more stop, just one more.

Don't die first.

The crowds were thick and got even thicker as he got closer to Central. He wove through them the best he could but then—wham!—the inevitable happened.

A woman ahead made a sudden left directly in front of him.

He tried to stop but couldn't but mowed her down from behind.

She hit the ground hard.

Two shopping bags and a purse flew.

Everyone in the area stopped.

The woman sat up, disoriented, holding her face.

Blood came from it, then tears.

That's when someone shouted something at Teffinger, something mean.

He bent down and helped the woman to her feet. "I am so sorry."

32

August 7
Friday Afternoon

By the end of the session, Kong was so horny that he took Kam Lee, right there on the rack, and took her hard even by his standards. Then they made drinks, headed for the pool out back, and sat in crystal clear water up to their chests. It was cooler than a hot tub but not by much.

"I'm being blackmailed," Kong said. "It's in connection with Destiny Ng Jun."

The shock on Kam Lee's face was palpable.

"Destiny Ng Jun? She was what—a year ago?"

Kong nodded.

"July 18."

She pressed for details.

Kong gave them.

The first call came two weeks after the fact, from a woman who said she was sitting in the shadows by the water watching the lights of Kowloon when a man and woman walked by. For some reason, things didn't seem right, so she studied them. Then something terrible happened. The man looked around, saw no one, and slit the woman's throat, just like that.

The woman grabbed the wound, staggered for a second, and dropped to the ground. The man threw a knife in the water. Then he picked the woman up, raised her over his head and threw her as far out as he could. She splashed. He looked around one more time, saw no one, and got the hell out of there.

"I followed you to the Causeway Bay Typhoon Shelter," the caller said. "You got in a dinghy and disappeared into the night. Two days later, there was a newspaper article about an 18-year-old woman named Destiny Ng Jun who was found floating in the harbour. The paper didn't say her throat had been slit, but I knew. That was wrong, what you did. Your prints are all over that knife. For your sake, I hope the police never find it. They won't, of course, unless someone tells them where to look."

Kong exhaled.

"We negotiated over the next couple of days," he said. "I tried to figure out who she was but got nowhere. Then I paid her. It was supposed to be a one-shot deal, after which she would go her way and I would go mine. She surfaced again out of the blue on Tuesday, demanding more money."

"Did you pay her?"

He nodded.

"I had no choice," he said. "She took me by surprise."

Kam Lee wrinkled her forehead.

"You should have told me right away, back when it first happened," she said.

Kong nodded.

That was true.

He didn't deny it.

"I was stupid," he said. "There was also another development, just a couple of hours ago." He told her about the woman who broke into Dangerous Lady, and the other one on shore who got away with his laptop. "My guess is that the one who went on the boat is the same one who's been blackmailing me. She was looking for more dirt. And now she has an accomplice, too. "

"So what do you want me to do—help you kill them?"

Kong shook his head.

"No, not kill them," he said, "just find them. I have a plan to figure out who they are, but I'll need your help. Once I have them identified, I'll take care of things from there. You won't need to do anything else."

Kam Lee clinked her glass against his.

"I'm in, but all the way, not just half," she said. "We should bring 'em back here and show 'em how pain works before we kill them."

Kong pictured it and didn't mind what he saw.

They deserved it.

"Now that I think of it, I have a client who would love to take it all the way," she said. "Maybe we should let him do it."

"You think?"

She nodded.

"He'd probably pay big dollars, too," she said. "You'd get your money back, or at least some of it. He'd take his time. I can already picture it. It gives me chills just thinking about it."

Kong cocked his head.

"Go ahead and feel him out, with no guarantees," he said. "Just be sure you keep things vague."

"He'll definitely want to do it," Kam Lee said. "There's no doubt in my mind. We'll even shut the place down so he's the only one here."

"What's his name?"

She ran a finger down his chest.

"You know I don't do that."

33

August 7
Friday Night

Friday night, the sun gave way to neon and the heat lost its stranglehold. Prarie and Emmanuelle took a double-decker bus north on Nathan Road, deep into Kowloon, and got off in Mangkok at Argyle Street. The rumor was that this was the most crowded real estate in the world; the golden mile.

Being here, right now, Prarie believed it.

Insane bumper-to-bumper traffic, four lanes wide, crawled along. Thousands of people congested the sidewalks, elbow to elbow. Neon signs were everywhere, not just flat against the buildings, but cantilevered over the street, as big and as far as their supports would go, creating a canopy of light.

"Somewhere there are three nuclear reactors going at full speed just to power this block," Emmanuelle said.

Prarie chuckled.

"I was going to guess four."

Every store was open.

The eateries and bars were jammed to the walls.

Prarie's purse seemed heavier then usual and then she remembered why—the knife. Emmanuelle's would even be heavier.

She had the gun, cleaned now, with six bullets left in the clip.

All of Emmanuelle's credit cards and identification papers were in her back pocket, however, not the purse. That way she could abandon it in a Hong Kong heartbeat if she needed to and not worry about getting traced to it.

The bar they were looking for turned out to be a loud, smoky, shoulder-to-shoulder place with a Filipino band, Grade-C, considerably drunker than it should be. They got drinks, found a place to stand and waited. When the men looked, it was usually at Prarie, who was more their size. Emmanuelle intimidated them. Ten minutes later a man walked up and said in English, "Are you the ladies who want the painting?"

He was young, about twenty-five, taller than average, nice looking and clean cut; not what Prarie expected.

"Yes," Emmanuelle said.

"I'm the artist," he said. "Come with me."

He led them out of the bar and off the beaten path, away from the neon, to a crappy car, and told them to get in the back. Then he handed them blindfolds and said, "Put these on."

Prarie's heart raced.

"Why?"

"Because no one gets to know where the studio is," he said. Prarie must have had a look on her face because the man added, "This is a deal-breaker."

Prarie looked at Emmanuelle who exhaled and put the blindfold on.

Prarie followed suit.

The car pulled away.

They drove for a long time. Based on the decreasing traffic congestion, they were probably going north. No one spoke. Ostensibly, all the cloak-and-dagger was to keep the location of the studio unknown, not only because of the inventory of replicas, but because the artist was also a collector.

He was ripe for the robbing if a robber knew where to look.

He took no chances.

"We're almost there," he said. "Two more minutes."

34

August 7
Friday Afternoon

After losing the trail of the mystery woman, Teffinger called Fan Rae and told her he just got a call from Denver and needed to handle an emergency matter this afternoon. A man charged with murder filed a motion to exclude evidence and the D.A. needed to email a number of documents to Teffinger and go over them.

That was a lie; a lie to avoid seeing Fan Rae until he could figure things out.

"We're still on for tonight, right?" she asked.

"Absolutely," he said. "I'll call you as soon as I'm free."

When he hung up, he called Dr. Leigh Sandt, the FBI profiler from Quantico, Virginia. She answered on the third ring, groggy, getting woken up. He pictured a classy lady sitting up in bed, about fifty, with the best legs in the universe—Tina Turner legs.

"It's me," he said.

"Nick?"

"Yeah."

"Do you know what time it is?"

He did a quick calculation.

It would be 4:00 a.m., Virginia time.

He should have waited three hours.

"Look, I know I'm waking you and I'm really sorry about it, but I have a situation," he said. "I didn't know who else to call."

"You sound faint," she said. "Where are you?"

"Hong Kong."

"Hong Kong?"

"Right."

"What are you doing in Hong Kong?"

"Hunting," he said. "But here's the thing. I'm working with a Hong Kong detective by the name of Fan Rae Fan. I just came across some information to the effect that she's actually connected to the people I'm looking for—I'm not sure yet if she's part of them or covering up for them or what. But I do know that she's dirty and she's lying to me. What I need is some background on her."

Silence.

"That would be a CIA matter," she said.

"I know," Teffinger said. "Can you make a call?"

Leigh grunted.

"God, Nick, if it was anyone but you—"

"Love you," he said.

"Be careful," she said. "It sounds like you're way out of your league."

"I usually am."

"I'll call you as soon as I know something," she said. "It may be a couple of days."

"I don't have a couple of days. I might not even have a couple of hours."

"Nothing's ever normal with you, Teffinger," she said. "Do you know that?"

Unfortunately, he did.

He spent the rest of the afternoon on the Star Ferry, ping-ponging across Victoria Harbour between Hong Kong and Kowloon, hoping that the salt air would clear his thoughts.

It did, to a point.

He was able to figure out a few things.

Fan Rae knew who d'Asia was, meaning she had been deceiving Teffinger by pretending she knew nothing. The reason she had been deceiving him was because the mystery woman was going to kill d'Asia. Fan Rae was either going to help her or, at a minimum, manipulate Teffinger until the deed was done.

Based on that information alone, Teffinger's opinion about Fan Rae should be easy—namely, that she was a woman he couldn't ever respect or love, not in a million years.

But there was a problem.

When they made love, it was real.

Fan Rae hadn't been faking it.

Nor had he.

As much as he wished he could, he couldn't turn off his feelings about her just because it made sense.

He still liked her and maybe even loved her.

There was one more problem, too, a big one—he still thought about d'Asia. He could still see feel her straddling him in the dark. He could still smell the rain in her hair. He could still taste her skin.

What to do?

What to do?

Dr. Leigh Sandt phoned just as dusk settled on Hong Kong and the neon lights started to flicker "I called in some markers and officially owe three blowjobs," she said. "Unfortunately, nothing bubbled to the surface. Based on what everyone could throw together fast, the woman is clean. That doesn't mean there isn't something there to find, given time and effort, but if it's there it's going to take some digging."

"Thanks."

He appreciated it.

He really did.

"You want us to dig deeper?"

Teffinger ran his fingers through his hair and pictured the process, namely surveillance, interviews, records searches, the kinds of things that took weeks.

"Hold off for now," he said. "Let me see how the next couple of days go."

"Okay."

"I owe you one," he said.

She laughed.

"Yeah, right, one—followed by two zeros."

"I didn't know you were keeping count," he said. "Next time you're in Denver, I'll take you out and get you drunk."

"Deal," she said. "At a cowboy bar. Do you still have some of those around?"

He did.

He did indeed.

"Okay then," Teffinger said. "I've got you penciled in."

"Oh, no, not pencil, buddy—pen. I know how your pencil works."

Fan Rae called ten minutes later.

"Are we still on for tonight?"

"Absolutely."

"I'll pick you up at 9:30," she said. "I'm wearing something dark so I don't stand out too much."

Teffinger thought, g-punk.

"Good idea," he said. "Just be sure it's something that comes off."

"Do you want me to wear pants or a dress?"

A dress, a short one.

The shortest one she has.

"What color underwear?"

"No underwear."

"You want me to wear the shortest dress I have and no underwear?"

"That's right."

"I didn't know you were so nasty," she said.

"Now you know."

"I've never done that before."

"Do it tonight."

"Why?"

"Because I asked you to. Show me I'm special."

"But you are special."

"Prove it."

Silence.

"Okay," she said, "but in return I expect you to get me seriously drunk."

"Done."

Teffinger hung up and didn't know why he did what he just did. Maybe it was to see what her limits were, and whether she'd go there for him. Maybe it was just so he could squeeze her bare ass whenever he felt like it.

"Don't over-think it," he muttered. "Your brain isn't that big."

35

August 7
Friday Night

Ra busted onto the SoHo scene eight months ago and became the instant big dog. It had a section for every sin. Paramount was an insanely massive techno dance floor with women in suspended cages who gyrated in their underwear. But there was also a live band room called the Inferno, a hostess bar called Twisted, and a bed and sofa lounge called Chills. Every nook and cranny was filled with sexual tension and the most beautiful people in Hong Kong.

Kong ran the place.

He was in charge of all hiring and firing, meaning no one worked there without his approval. He personally chose the bartenders, doormen, dancers, and everyone else. Only the pretty needed to apply. He was also present most nights, with his smiles and rock star looks and perfect clothes seductively unbuttoned, to be sure that the customers had a good time, with particular attention to the GQ, the models and the rich and relevant.

His job sounded easy.

It wasn't, anything but.

He earned his money.

Behind him, in the background, was an army of geeks who handled the mundane, things like ads and promotion, booking the bands, liquor inventory, security, insurance, bookkeeping, licensing, housekeeping, maintenance, payroll, benefits, taxes, et cetera.

Jack Poon owned the place.

It was a drop in his bucket.

It could evaporate and his bottom line wouldn't even twitch.

Kong had been managing a smaller club in Lan Quai Fong called Freefall, also a Poon club although no one knew it, and got moved over to Ra when it opened. Kong didn't meet Poon for five months and even that was just a quick handshake.

Poon didn't micro-manage.

He delegated and then disappeared.

Friday night was the big one at Ra, the party night.

Kong got there early, an hour before the club opened.

Good thing, too.

Problems were already in the making.

Shortly after midnight, something unexpected happened. Jack Poon showed up, in the flesh. That by itself would have provided cause to take notice. To add to the spectacle, however, his slender frame was sandwiched between two women, both western, both blond, both a good six inches taller than him, both drop-dead gorgeous.

Everyone in the club stared.

Most didn't know who he was, at least by sight, but everyone knew one thing—he had deep pockets, lots and lots of deep pockets.

For that reason alone, people parted as he walked.

Kong hustled his way over to see if the man needed liquor or a roped-off booth or private room to screw his lovelies or whatever.

"Actually, I swung by to talk to you," Poon said. "Remember that new plan that I was going to work on?"

Kong remembered and nodded.

"Well, I think I came up with something." He slapped Kong on the back and said, "You're going to be in awe. It makes that airplane thing look like a day at the zoo."

Kong swallowed, both excited and repulsed.

"No parachutes, right?" he asked.

Poon grinned and said, "You're too much." Then he handed one of the blonds to him and said, "This one's for you. Let's sit down somewhere and have a drink."

They ended up in the hostess room, Twisted, at the booth in the back corner. Poon ordered six women, shoved money in their crotches and got them drunk. Then he positioned them as a visual wall around the perimeter of the table and motioned for the blonds to get underneath.

They did.

Kong felt his zipper slide down.

Poon cocked his head and said, "The rules are simple. Keep your hands on the table. The first one who comes is the loser."

36

August 7
Friday Night

Two minutes after the artist said "Two minutes," the vehicle came to a stop and the engine shut off. Prarie reached up to uncover her eyes when a vice-like hand wrapped around her wrist and brought it down.

"Leave the blindfolds on until we get inside."

"Why?"

"Just humor me," he said. "It's only a few more minutes."

He led them out of the car and through a door.

"Okay, you can take them off," he said.

Prarie expected to be in a studio, standing in the midst of paintings. But she was in a dark industrial warehouse, mostly empty and gutted, but with scattered silhouettes of ancient machinery here and there. Two sturdy wooden chairs sat on the concrete in front of her. Each had rope tied on the arms and legs, where a person's wrists and ankles would be.

The man looked at Emmanuelle first, then Prarie, and said, "You are very stupid ladies."

Suddenly a second person grabbed Emmanuelle from behind.

It was a man, a strong man.

She screamed.

The scream stopped when the man brought a cloth to her mouth and pulled it against her face.

She struggled violently.

It did no good.

Then she dropped to the ground.

At the same time someone grabbed Prarie from behind, a third man.

A terrible saturated cloth came to her mouth.

Her first instinct was to grab the man's hand and pull it off, but she couldn't. Then she dropped straight down, slithered out from under his arms and rolled when she hit the ground. Something was there next to her—Emmanuelle's purse.

The man came at her as a cat would a mouse, slowly, enjoying the anticipation.

"So, you want to play?" he said.

Before she knew it, the gun was in her hand.

The man by Emmanuelle saw it and charged with a knife.

Fast.

With obvious intent.

She fired.

Bam!

Bam!.

He dropped to the ground, twitched, gurgled and then stopped moving.

The other man came at her.

The cat.

She turned the gun on him.

"Stop right there!"

He hesitated, as if deciding, and then stopped.

The air was deathly silent.

No one said a word.

Not a sound came from anywhere, other than the air passing in and out of everyone's lungs.

37

August 7
Friday Night

Wearing a short black dress and matching high heels, Fan Rae picked Teffinger up at the Fleming after dark and headed east on Hennessy Road towards the Wan Chai district. The garment rode up as she drove, dangerously high, and the smooth golden skin of her thighs occasionally flashed with a neon blue or green or yellow. Fan Rae must have caught him staring because she said, "I did what you wanted."

"You mean the panties?"

She nodded.

"Lack thereof, to be precise," she said. "Go ahead and check."

He almost did, but said, "Later."

"You're such a tease." She exhaled. "Hong Kong nights get me horny. They're the best in the world. I've been to a lot of places—Bangkok, Tokyo, Rome, Paris—none of them compare."

"Have you ever been to the United States?"

She shook her head.

"No interest," she said.

Minutes later they were on Queens Road East, pulling into the parking lot of a standalone building with a neon sign that said High Tide Bar.

"We're here," she said.

A large number of women were inside, all young, all beautiful, all professional flirts. From what Fan Rae told Teffinger earlier, most of the hostess girls in Hong Kong were now from the Philippines or Thailand. Their main function was to fawn over the men, get them drunk, feed them fruit, sing Karaoke, rub their legs and laugh heartily at anything that was even remotely funny.

They were adorable young women spending time with older, not-so-adorable guys.

For that, the men paid roughly $500 HKD per hour per girl.

Plus the bar tab.

Plus tips.

Many of the men were Chinese businessmen who came to close deals and show respect to their counterparts by spending money on them. In those situations, the girls were careful to not favor one man over another, as such would be an act of disrespect.

Then there were the westerners, expats and weary travelers, looking for a little company and hoping there would at least be an under-the-table handjob at the end of it all.

There wouldn't be.

There was no sex, not in the club anyway.

Many of the women though wrote down their phone numbers for after-hours services, off-site.

One Girl, One Room.

That was the most popular form of prostitution in Hong Kong, meaning one woman with her own, private apartment.

No pimps.

No hotels.

The High Tide Bar, like most hostess bars, started life at a topless bar. Then there came a point when licenses were no longer given out. The topless bars eventually disappeared as they were traded or sold. Hostess bars sprang up in their stead as the next best thing.

Teffinger and Fan Rae took a booth. A few minutes later, a classy woman named Sun An joined them. She was old enough that she was clearly not one of the girls but probably had been ten years ago.

"Would you like me to send a girl over?" she asked.

Fan Rae nodded.

"Yes, Syling Wu," she said.

Sun Ah frowned.

"Syling has not shown up yet."

"Is she scheduled?"

"She is."

"When was she supposed to be here?"

Sun Ah looked at her watch.

"An hour ago."

"Is she usually late?"

No.

Never.

Not even five minutes.

This was very unlike her.

"Did she call in?"

No.

She didn't.

"We'll wait for a little and see if she shows up," Fan Rae said.

Sun Ah patted her hand and said, "Fine. In the meantime, would you like someone else to join you?"

"Yes, please."

"Do you see one in particular that you'd like?"

Fan Rae looked at Teffinger and said, "You choose."

Teffinger surveyed the landscape and said, "Who would Syling want here, if she shows up and joins us?"

"Probably her," Sun Ah said, nodding.

"Okay then," Teffinger said. "Her."

Teffinger had to admit, the woman who joined them—a 21-year-old Bangkok girl named Dan Dan—would have been enticing to a man who was looking for nothing other than youth and beauty. She was too young for Teffinger's taste, though, and he wished she was in a dorm room studying for a test instead of sitting here with her hand on his knee.

They ordered drinks.

Sun Ah set an entire bottle on the table, plus three

glasses.

Teffinger must have had a look on his face because Fan Rae whispered in his ear, "I got the tab, so relax."

"You sure?"

She nodded.

"I'll be reimbursed," she said. "This is work."

Okay.

Good.

Dan Dan had big brown eyes, a fashionably distressed hairdo, a floral silk blouse hugging a buxom chest, and a white miniskirt. She started off perky, in character, but got serious when they told her they were detectives and wanted to know about Syling Wu.

"She just up and vanished," Dan Dan said.

She no longer answered her phone.

She wasn't at her apartment.

None of her friends had seen her.

No one had heard from her.

She didn't show up for work tonight.

"And here's something else weird," Dan Dan said. "A man was in here earlier tonight looking for her and wanting to know if anyone knew where she was. The guy gave me the creeps."

"What was his name?"

"He never told me," Dan Dan said. "Something happened to Syling. I don't know if this creepy guy was part of it or what. But something definitely happened to her. She's g-punk—not here of course, on her own time—but she's stable and dependable."

Teffinger raked his fingers through his hair.

"Describe this guy," he said. "The creep."

She did.

He was about fifty, Chinese, five-three and slight of build. "There was something wrong with his eyes."

"You mean physically wrong?"

"No, more like the brain behind those eyes was—what?—I don't know, twisted or something."

"Would you recognize the guy, if you saw him again?"

Dan Dan nodded.

Definitely.

In a heartbeat.

Teffinger was about questioned out when one more popped into his head. "Was Syling into pagan practices or anything like that?"

Dan Dan shook her head.

"No," she said.

"Is that the kind of thing you would know about, if it was happening?"

"I think so."

"Did Syling ever go to a bar called Hei Yewan?"

"Yes."

"Yes?"

Dan Dan nodded.

"Yes, probably once a month or thereabouts. It's a g-punk hangout."

"Did she ever go to the back room of that place?"

The woman looked confused.

"I didn't know there was a back room."

"Syling never said anything about a back room that has a K'ung chia symbol painted on the floor?"

No.

She didn't.

"Is that why she's gone?" Dan Dan asked. "Because of that room?"

Teffinger shrugged.

"We don't know," he said. "Do you know Nuwa Moon?"

"I know she's Syling's friend but I never met her."

Fan Rae paid the bill, a big bill. She gave Dan Dan a sizeable tip, plus her business card in case she thought of anything else. Then they headed for Hei Yewan, mingled with the crowd and showed pictures of Nuwa Moon and Syling Wu. What they found out was pretty much what Teffinger expected.

Both of the women had been there Wednesday night, the night Nuwa Moon got a symbol carved in her stomach. Unfortunately, however, no one knew or at least wouldn't talk about what was going on in the back room that night.

They left.

Fan Rae drove.

The neon city rolled by.

"Here's the way I see it," Teffinger said. "They were both there Wednesday night. They were in the main bar area the whole night, based on all the sightings. Whatever was going on in the back room, I don't think they knew about it or participated in it. Somehow, though, they got targeted. They left together and then got taken, probably by whoever was in that back room. Nuwa Moon ended up getting murdered.

That happened on the beach, not in the back room." A beat then, "What happened to Syling, I don't know. Maybe she was killed the same way someplace else."

Back at Fan Rae's apartment, Teffinger realized he had gone the whole night without lifting up her dress, so he did it now.

True to her word, she wasn't wearing any underwear.

"See, I proved it," she said. "You're special."

Teffinger walked her to the wall, pulled her arms up high and held them in place with one hand. With the other one, he reached down between her legs.

She spread her feet, trembled, and surrendered to his touch.

"I hate that you can do this to me," she said.

DAY SIX

August 8
Saturday

38

August 8
Saturday Morning

Prarie twisted and turned all night, a captive in that eerie netherworld where she wasn't quite asleep and wasn't quite awake. She woke Saturday morning in a seedy room—definitely not the InterContinental. She rolled over and stretched, hoping that the nasty thoughts about killing a man last night would evaporate like bad dreams do.

But they didn't.

Next to her, Emmanuelle breathed deep and heavy, soundly asleep.

She rolled out of bed, stepped into the shower and replayed the events of last night.

After she shot the man with the knife, things got real dicey real fast and, in hindsight, could have gone either way. But she had the gun and somehow kept her wits. She made one of the men tie the other one to one of the chairs. She gathered up their wallets, cell phones and knives, which went into her purse.

She made the man carry Emmanuelle outside.

A white BMW sat next to the junker they came in.

The keys were in the ignition.

She made the man put Emmanuelle in the back seat.

She debated briefly about shooting the two men who were left. Then she said, "Consider yourself lucky," and got the hell out of there.

Emmanuelle didn't wake up for a full hour.

When she did, and got the story, she said, "You're nicer than me. I would have killed them." She pointed to her forehead. "Right there. Bam bam, bye bye."

"I thought about it," Prarie said.

"You should have done it. Now we got to worry about them."

"Who are they?"

"My guess? They're after the paintings. Somehow they figured out we are too, probably from that gallery guy. He must have figured out that we were hunting for someone talented enough to make the fakes that got put into Musee d'Orsay. Then he tipped these guys off, or who knows, maybe he's even part of them. Either way, they lured us to that warehouse to find out what we know and we fell for it. I'll tell you one thing, I won't be that stupid again. Not even close."

To avoid problems, at least for the night, they used cash to check into a seedy place called the Sea View Hotel on the far eastern edge of Hong Kong, not far from the Wholesale Fish Market. Then they drove to North Point, abandoned the BMW behind a bar, and hoofed it back to the hotel.

That was last night.

Now it was morning.

Emmanuelle was awake when Prarie got out of the shower. She rubbed sleep from her eyes, hugged Prarie briefly, and said, "I want to work their cell phones this morning before they get smart and cut the service off. Chances are they know things we don't. We need to make a record of who they've been in touch with."

Prarie agreed.

"Do me a favor while I'm in the shower and figure out which one belongs to the dead guy," she added.

"Why?"

"Once the police found his body, they'll be tracking his phone," she said. "I don't want them zeroing in on us by GPS or something."

Prarie shook her head.

"How do you come up with this stuff?"

"I don't know. It's just there."

Emmanuelle headed to the shower.

Prarie headed outside for coffee and food. There would probably be something down by the fish market.

What she saw outside she could hardly believe.

A number of police cars were congregated not more than fifty meters down the road. Her natural instinct was to run, but she didn't, and on further examination saw that their interest was in something on the ground. Against her better judgment, she walked over.

On the ground was a body, not just any body, the body of the man she shot last night.

A small, meaty cop raised his eyes and looked at her briefly.

Then went back to work.

When Prarie got back to the hotel, Emmanuelle was still in the shower. Prarie pulled the curtain open and shook the woman by the arm. Emmanuelle jumped, then studied Prarie's face and said, "What's wrong?"

"The man I shot is on the ground, right down the street."

"You're kidding, right?"

No.

She wasn't.

"I don't get it," Prarie said.

Emmanuelle didn't either and wrinkled her forehead to prove it. Then the confusion disappeared.

"They dumped him there as a warning to us."

"Warning? What kind of warning?"

"A warning that they're not backing off and that we'd better cooperate."

"But how did they even find us?"

"My guess is the BMW, it probably has a GPS tracking system that showed them everywhere we went." She rinsed off what soap was left and said, "Hand me that towel. We need to get out of here."

"What do we do with the gun? It's still in my purse—"

"Bring it," Emmanuelle said. "We can't leave it here." Prarie must have had a deer-in-headlights look because Emmanuelle said, "Put it in my purse. I'll carry it."

Five minutes later they walked out of the hotel and nonchalantly headed in the direction away from the body.

They didn't turn around.

A hundred steps later, just when they were starting to feel safe, something bad happened. A cop car pulled up next to them and the cop said something in Cantonese.

"English," Prarie said.

He brought the car to a stop and stepped out.

He was small, meaty and mean looking.

Prarie recognized him as the one who looked up at her back by the body.

This time he addressed them in English.

"I want to talk to you two for a minute."

39

August 8
Saturday Morning

Fan Rae Fan was a drug and Teffinger was addicted. He realized that now as he got out of bed Saturday morning and saw the sensuous curves of her body once again. She was no good for him. She was implicated in the plan to kill d'Asia but he couldn't stay away, physically or emotionally. Each time he was with her, her pull became more powerful.

An explosive ending was inevitable.

He didn't want to think about it.

He dressed, gave her an imperceptible kiss as she slept, then headed for the door. He was in the hallway and about to close the door when he remembered her words.

Next time wake me.

He debated for a second, then went back in, laid down next to her and ran his fingers through her hair until she woke up. She kissed him as soon as she realized she was awake.

"I'm going to head back to the hotel for a jog and fresh clothes," he said. "I'll be back in an hour or two."

She put a finger on his lips.

He kissed it.

"You woke me," she said. "Thanks."

"I said I would."

"I know, but I didn't know if you would," she said. "When you get back to the hotel, check out and bring your stuff over here. Stay with me. I don't like being away from you."

Teffinger stood up.

"If I do, you'll need to devote a whole cabinet to coffee," he said. "You realize that, I hope."

Fan Rae insisted that he use her car, so he did, punching the radio buttons and actually getting a Beatles song.

"I Call Your Name."

At the Fleming, he searched the car to see if there were any leads as to who the mystery woman was, the one who was going to kill d'Asia.

If the clues were there, they didn't jump out.

Nada.

Nothing.

Once he moved in with Fan Rae, he'd be able to search her apartment. Maybe his luck would be better there.

He bypassed the elevator, took the stairwell to his room, and then set out for a good jog through the

Hong Kong cityscape, keeping up the pace and fighting the humidity. He needed more of this, a lot more. There was a time when he worked out five days a week without missing and had a six-pack to prove it. That changed when he got promoted to the head of the homicide unit three years ago. Most people considered him to be in phenomenal shape, but if you asked him, he was soft.

Back at the hotel room, he did five sets of fifty pushups alternated with five sets of a hundred stomach crunches and then took a long cool shower.

When he got out, someone knocked on the door, timidly, barely perceptible.

He wrapped a towel around his waist and opened the door.

Standing in front of him was the last person he expected.

D'Asia.

40

August 8
Saturday Morning

Kong woke Saturday morning when a throaty go-fast motored up to the port side of Dangerous Lady and someone jumped aboard. Kong looked out the portal, saw the Predator, and was informed that he had been summoned to Poon's penthouse. When he got there, Poon introduced him to a man with a stressed face, about 45, rough, with an iron handshake.

Vance Wu.

"Vance is a friend of mine," Poon explained. "He came to me this morning with some very bad news. He has a daughter named Syling Wu, she's 21. On Wednesday night, she went to a club called Hei Yewan, which is a g-punk hangout. She went with a friend named Nuwa Moon. Did you hear about the woman who was found floating down by the piers?"

Kong nodded.

He had, but hadn't paid much attention.

"That was Nuwa Moon," Poon said. "Someone killed her. Mr. Wu's daughter, Syling, has not been seen or heard from since Wednesday night."

"That's rough," Kong said.

Poon nodded.

"Yes, rough," Poon said. "Mr. Wu came to me, asking for help. Now I'm coming to you. What I need you to do is help find Syling Wu."

Kong shifted his weight.

"That's a job for a P.I., or even more to the point—the police," he said. "Not to mention, I don't have the skills."

Poon looked out the window, then back at Kong. "Mr. Wu already has an investigator on it," Poon said. "Unfortunately, he's not the best. In fact, he comes across sort of creepy. Later this morning he's going to be fired and replaced with someone infinitely better, a woman I know by the name of Brittany So Kwok. She'll take the lead. What I want you to do is be at her disposal. If she calls you and asks to get something done, it needs to get done."

"You mean dirty stuff," Kong said.

Poon shrugged.

"Whatever," he said. "We're not going to have time to obey all the laws, or play nicey-nice with everybody, or leave it to unmotivated and underpaid civil servants. We need speed. We need someone who can cut through the crap and get the job done. A facilitator, if you will."

"Why the rush? Do you think she's still alive?"

Wu grabbed Kong's arm.

"She's alive," he said. He pounded his heart. "I can feel her, in here."

Kong nodded.

Okay.

Fine.

Who was he to argue?

"Once we find out who took her, there's going to be some sanitation work to do."

Kong studied the man.

"What makes you think I would do something like that?"

Poon smiled.

"Why? Am I wrong?"

"I didn't say you were wrong."

"Okay then," Poon said. "We appreciate your help. To show our appreciation, you're going to be paid well."

Kong smiled.

"Sounds reasonable," he said.

Poon handed him an envelope.

"Good faith money," he said. "Discretion is of the utmost importance. I'm sure you appreciate that."

Kong did.

"Be sure Brittany So Kwak doesn't get hurt."

Kong nodded.

"I would be most unpleased if she got hurt," Poon added. Then he slapped Kong on the back. "You like the Predator? It's a nice boat, huh? Slices right through the chop."

"Yes it does."

Kong was almost out the door when Poon grabbed his arm and said, "One more thing. You'll find Brittany to be a very attractive lady. She's here to do a job, not to be screwed, so be sure you keep it that way."

"Is she a girlfriend of yours?"

Poon laughed.

"All the women in Hong Kong are my girlfriends of mine, even the ones who don't know it yet," he said. "Maybe someday you'll have real money and understand what I'm talking about."

"I already have real money."

Poon shook his head.

"What you have is Saturday night fun money," he said. "But maybe things will get better for you. Who knows?"

41

August 8
Saturday Morning

The meaty, mean-looking cop asked Prarie and Emmanuelle if they stayed at the Sea View Hotel last night and, when they said "Yes," wanted to know if they saw or heard anything.

No.

Sorry.

He took a curious look at the way Emmanuelle clutched her purse, and said, "Okay, thanks."

He never asked their names.

They took the MRT to Central where there were a billion people around in case the cops traced a phone signal. They turned on the dead man's cell, copied everything in the memory—especially recent calls to and from—turned it off, and then did the same with the other two. They took the Star Ferry across the harbour, went to the far end of the boat, made sure no one was looking, and dropped all three of them over the side.

The deep choppy water swallowed them instantly.

"What about the gun?" Prarie asked.

Good question.

They had debated it all morning—it saved their lives once and gave them an edge for the future, but it also connected them to a murder and was illegal as hell.

Now it was time to decide once and for all.

"We have four bullets left," Emmanuelle said. "You decide."

"You sure?"

"Yes."

They wiped it for prints one more time, made sure no eyes were on them, dropped it over the side and watched it disappear into the salty green water.

There.

Done.

"I feel a hundred times better," Prarie said.

"Yeah," Emmanuelle said, but there was no conviction in her voice.

The knife-wielding maniac who forced Prarie to shoot him last night turned out to be Pierre Durand, 37, from Paris, according to his wallet. The other two were Nicholas Lefebvre, 32, also from Paris, and Michael Chow, 25, from Hong Kong. "We need to figure out if they're a group trying to find the paintings or the ones who took them in the first place," Emmanuelle said.

"How do we do that?" Prarie asked.

Good question.

"As far as our two Paris boys go, I know a P.I. back home who isn't above breaking into a flat or two if the money's good enough," Emmanuelle said. "The problem in this case, though, is that it's so sensitive. If I tell this guy to look around for something connected to paintings, he might put two and two together, which wouldn't be good."

"You don't think he can be trusted?"

Emmanuelle tilted her head.

"With normal stuff, yes, but with something this big, no one can be trusted," she said. "Everyone becomes a player."

Prarie considered it.

Then she said, "Maybe we need to go back to Paris and do it ourselves."

"You mean, break in?"

"Right."

Emmanuelle shrugged.

"It's a possibility but it'll take time," she said. "Maybe what I can do is keep it vague, so he doesn't know what he's looking for. I can just tell him to gather up papers and copy computer files, assuming there are computers, and then send it all to us."

"What kind of papers?"

"The normal stuff—bank statements, phone records, et cetera. Even then, he might spot something he shouldn't." She cocked her head. "Yeah, I'll do that and just hope it doesn't come back to bite us. In the meantime, let's concentrate on our Hong Kong friend."

Michael Chow.

42

August 8
Saturday Morning

The sight of d'Asia's face brought it all back—the rain, the blond-wig attacker, the body dump, and most of all the incredible passionate moments when she tried to lead him into the bedroom..

Moments that changed his life.

Inside the hotel room, d'Asia wrapped her arms around Teffinger's waist and laid her head on his chest.

Safe.

Protected.

"I shouldn't have come here," she said. "If someone follows me, you could be in trouble."

"How did you even know I was here?" Teffinger asked.

"I could feel you in the city and started calling hotels," she said.

"You could feel me?"

She nodded.

"Don't ask me to explain it," she said. "Nothing like this has ever happened to me before." She kissed him and said, "I can't believe you came all this way."

Teffinger exhaled.

"I didn't think I'd find you," he said.

"Technically you didn't," she said. "I found you."

Teffinger rolled his eyes.

"So you're a better detective than me? Is that what you're saying?"

She smiled.

"Yes, but don't worry, you're still young—you'll improve. Maybe if you're good, I'll show you some of my tricks." She ran a finger in tingly circles around his bellybutton. Then she grabbed the towel and yanked it off. "One of us is naked," she said.

"That's an uneven situation," Teffinger said.

"It is."

"It upsets the balance of the universe."

"It does."

"That's not good."

"So how are you going to fix it?"

Every molecule in his body screamed for him to throw the woman on the bed and rock her world like no one ever had, even him.

But it wasn't that simple.

Fan Rae pulled at him, hard and forcefully. Just a couple of hours ago, she asked him to move in. Also just a couple of hours ago, he said yes. He didn't know exactly what that meant as far as a commitment went, but did know that it meant something. And he knew for certain that sleeping with d'Asia would be a violation of whatever that something was.

Damn it.

He picked the towel off the floor and wrapped it around his waist as d'Asia watched with confusion.

"It's not that I don't want to," he said. "I do, more than you can even believe."

She raised her arms, put her hands around his neck and brought her mouth close to his, so close that the warmth of her breath filled his world. She rubbed her stomach against his and said, "What's wrong? Don't you like me anymore?"

Teffinger exhaled.

"Let's talk," he said.

Over the next half hour, he learned a few things. After returning to Hong Kong, d'Asia went into hiding, deep hiding, while a P.I. she hired by the name of Sammy Tsng tried to figure out what was going on.

So far he didn't know squat.

He had however worked hard and used up the retainer.

Now he needed more money.

"I never stopped thinking about you Nick," d'Asia said, "not for a moment. I almost jumped on a plane to Denver fifty different times but each time I reminded myself that I'd ruined your life enough."

Teffinger put his finger to her lips.

"Nothing was your fault," he said. "I think I know who's trying to kill you—or at least one of them—I don't know how many there are."

She studied him.

Then she said, "You're actually serious."

He nodded.

"Dead."

"You know who's trying to kill me?"

"Yes," he said. "Weird, isn't it? I couldn't find you, but did find out who's after you."

"Well, spit it out," she said. "Who is it?"

He started at the beginning.

Rather than reporting the incident to the Lakewood P.D., he dumped the woman with the wig near some railroad tracks in Denver after d'Asia ran out of the house. That way he'd have jurisdiction over the case and would get cooperation from the Hong Kong authorities when he came here. He'd been working with a detective named Fan Rae Fan since he arrived.

"We sort of developed a thing," he said.

"You've only been here a few days."

"Yeah, I know."

"And?"

"And what?"

"And is thing serious?"

Teffinger raked his hair back with his fingers. It immediately flopped back down over his forehead.

"This thing is on a path of self-destruction," he said, "because she's involved with the people who are trying to kill you, although I don't know exactly how. I'm still trying to figure it out."

With that, he told her the story of the conversation he overhead at Hei Yewan, and how he tried to follow the mystery woman.

"Describe this woman," she said.

He did.

She listened, solemnly.

"Do you know her?" he asked.

She shook her head.

"I might if I saw her, but not by that description," she said. "So what do we do?"

Easy.

She would stay in hiding.

Teffinger would stick by Fan Rae and wait for the mystery woman to surface.

"Are you going to be sleeping with this detective—this Fan Rae Fan?"

Teffinger shrugged.

"I don't know."

"Meaning you might?"

"Right, I guess so."

She cocked her head. "You know something? I had you all wrong."

"What does that mean."

"It means that Fan Rae Fan is the enemy," she said. "Staying close to the enemy to get information is one thing. Sleeping with the enemy is something entirely different."

Teffinger considered it.

He couldn't argue but he also knew that he couldn't promise he wouldn't sleep with Fan Rae.

She was in his blood, for better or worse.

He had fallen for the wrong woman.

He knew it.

He still couldn't do anything about it.

"How can I trust you if you're sleeping with the enemy?" d'Asia asked.

"I'd never do anything to hurt you. You know that."

She studied him, headed to the door and said, "I need to think this through."

Then she was gone, again.

43

August 8
Saturday Morning

The saltwater had some chop, but not enough for the Predator to notice as it sliced through Victoria Harbour. Kong stood up and let the wind blow in his face. He had to admit, the boat was nice—big, fast, strong, loud, sexy. Most guys thought it was macho. Kong didn't. Macho wasn't standing at a throttle, no matter how much boat was connected to it. Macho was untying a sailboat and pointing it straight into the meat of a storm.

He felt good.

No, not good.

GOOD.

Jack Poon had taken him into his trust, which would ultimately mean riches beyond Kong's wildest imagination. He'd need to earn it, sure, but that was just a matter of performance. Don't screw up any of the front-end projects; that's what he needed to concentrate on.

It would be interesting to see what this P.I. wanted him to do.

This woman named Brittany So Kwak.

The one he wasn't supposed to screw.

A Star Ferry crossed in front of them, a couple hundred meters ahead, and threw out a good-sized wake.

The Predator would get airborne.

Kong held on.

The man at the wheel said, "Oh yeah, baby!"

He hammered the throttle.

The front end of the boat jumped when it hit the wave and the engines whined as the props got dangerously close to breaking the surface.

The guy at the wheel grinned at Kong and hollered.

Then, wham!

The boat pounded down and headed for the second part of the wake, coming off the starboard side.

No problem.

Kong looked at the ferry.

What he saw he could hardly believe.

Two women were near the stern, dropping what looked to be a gun into the water and watching it disappear. Even at a distance, Kong recognized the taller woman—the blond—as the one who pulled his computer out of the dinghy and ran. The other woman had the same size and posture as the woman who broke into his boat and then disappeared after she rounded the pier.

Kong grabbed the arm of the man behind the wheel.

The noise of the hull pounding against the chop was deafening.

Kong had to shout to get his voice over it.

"Drop me off over there!"

"What?"

Kong pointed to the left and said, "Drop me off over there!"

"You don't want to go to the sailboat?"

"No, go over there! Kowloon!"

They flew over the second part of the wake, crashed back to the water, and then carved to the left.

Kong kept his eyes on the women.

You two want to play?

Fine.

Let's play.

44

August 8
Saturday Morning

Michael Chow lived in North Point, five kilometers east of Central, in Flat 18, 1F, Coronet Court, 321 King's Road. Like most Hong Kong streets, the place was jammed with shops, people, vehicles and signs. A waist-high guardrail separated the sidewalk from the street. The flats were piled up for several stories above the shops and looked just as busy as the street itself. Air conditioners stuck out everywhere and hummed with a mean persistency. The entrance was an inconspicuous door sandwiched between two shops. Prarie and Emmanuelle walked into that entrance and rang the buzzer for Chow's flat.

No answer.

They pressed it again.

Same thing.

"What do you think?" Emmanuelle asked.

Prarie shifted her feet.

"We've come this far."

They headed up.

They didn't encounter a lot of people on the way, but the ones they did meet gave them an extra curious stare.

They were western.

The building wasn't the Ritz.

They knocked on Chow's door.

No one answered.

The doorknob was locked and wouldn't turn, but the door hadn't been pulled shut all the way and the latch hadn't caught. When they pushed, it actually swung in. They stepped inside and closed it solidly behind them. The place was scorching in spite of the air conditioner.

It was small, too.

They didn't talk and set to work.

Prarie downloaded computer files while Emmanuelle shuffled through papers. They hadn't been at it for more than five minutes when a noise came from the door.

They froze.

Someone outside was sticking a key in the lock.

"Someone's coming!"

Prarie looked around for something to fight with. Anything.

She grabbed a pair of scissors.

Two seconds later, the door opened.

A woman walked in, stopped in her tracks and

said something in Cantonese. She was in her early twenties, timid, slender and conservatively dressed in shorts and sandals. She didn't have the look of a person involved in something desperate or illegal.

She looked innocent.

"Speak in English," Emmanuelle said.

The woman switched to English.

"Who are you?"

"Friends of Michael's," Emmanuelle said. "Who are you?"

"His girlfriend," she said. "How did you get in here?"

Emmanuelle sat down on the couch and motioned for the woman to join her.

"Let's talk for a minute."

45

August 8
Saturday Morning

Teffinger knew d'Asia wouldn't come back but hung around for an hour anyway before checking out and heading down to the car. The more he thought about it, the more he saw her point. He wouldn't trust anyone either if they were sleeping with the enemy.

He was halfway to Fan Rae's when he realized something bad.

D'Asia never asked for his number.

Teffinger didn't have hers.

He didn't know where she was staying, other than down deep. Hell, he didn't even know her last name. He turned around, headed back to the Fleming and checked back into his room. The guy at the reception desk gave him a curious glance and then kept all expressions off his face.

"Welcome back to the Fleming, Mr. Teffinger."

"Thanks," he said. "It's good to finally be back. It

doesn't look like much has changed since the last time I was here."

There.

Done.

This way, if d'Asia needed to contact him, she'd at least have a place to leave a message.

He must have had a look on his face when he got to Fan Rae's flat because she asked, "What's wrong?"

"Nothing."

She studied him and said, "Okay, be that way."

"Honest, nothing's wrong."

"Fine."

He ran his fingers through his hair.

"Okay, there is one thing."

"I knew it—"

"I don't think your friend from work likes me," he said, "the one who stopped in at Hei Yewan. She barely even looked at me when she left."

Fan Rae paused.

Then she said, "Don't take it personal. She's like that."

"So what's her story?"

Fan Rae cocked her head. "Why? Do you like her?"

He shrugged.

"No, it's just that she seemed interesting," he said. "Maybe we should go out for a drink tonight and invite her along. I'm sure she has some good stories to tell about you."

Fan Rae rolled her eyes.

"Where are you going with this, Nick? Are you looking for a threesome?"

He held up his hands in defense.

"No, not at all—"

She put a finger on his lips. "I don't mind, if you want to," she said. "I've done them before. But it can't be with anyone from work. I'm sure you understand why."

Then something unexpected happened.

Fan Rae said, "So we can bring her along if you want, but you only get me at the end of the evening."

"Trust me, you're all I want," he said.

He kissed her to prove it.

Then he said, "I need coffee."

She did too so they headed out.

On the way he said, "Were you serious about that threesome?"

"Dead."

"I like a woman every now and then," she said. "I guess it's time you knew that. In fact, the more I think about it, we should definitely do it. I want you to know who I am, deep down. If it turns out that you're not going to like me, I'd rather know it sooner than later."

"We're way past that," Teffinger said, and meant it.

"I know someone," Fan Rae said. "I think you'll like her. She smells like flowers."

Flowers.

There was nothing wrong with flowers—bouquets of flower, fields of flowers, they were all good.

"Afterwards, we'll all get matching tattoos," she said.

"Are you serious?"

She nodded.

"Something small and quick, just a memento."

She looked at him.

"I've never gotten a tattoo," he said.

"Well, I guess what you need to ask yourself is whether the time has come."

He thought about it.

The answer surprised him

"Okay," he said.

"Are you sure?"

"Yes. Positive."

She looped her arm through his. "You got me all hot," she said. "I want to do it tonight—the threesome and the tattoo. This is perfect, with today being Saturday."

"What about your friend from work?"

"We'll meet with her earlier, if she's available."

"Okay."

"She's sort of cute, don't you think?"

He did.

He did indeed.

"We'll use her to get you all hot and bothered," Fan Rae said. "Then we'll cut her loose and move on to the you-know-what."

That sounded reasonable, so reasonable that he picked Fan Rae up with one arm and swung her around until they both got dizzy.

"No flowers," he said.

"What do you mean?"

"The tattoo. I can't be running around with a flower on me."

Fan Rae laughed at the thought.

"Actually, I think a flower would be befitting."

Teffinger cocked his head.

Maybe she was right.

He ducked inside a small eatery for coffee. When he got out, Fan Rae had a grin on her face. "I made the calls," she said. "It's all set up."

Cool

Very cool.

"I'm going to get seriously drunk tonight and enjoy every minute of it," she said.

46

August 8
Saturday Morning

Kong was already on shore, waiting and watching fifty meters from the pier, when the two women got off the Star Ferry. He expected them to hop on a bus up Nathan Road but they walked over to the InterContinental Hotel instead.

He followed and then waited outside, at first for a half hour, then for an hour.

The sun rose higher and trained every ounce of its energy directly on Kong, heating him up, frying his brain. He needed air conditioning; not in ten minutes, now, right this second. Two minutes later he pushed through revolving doors and into an opulent lobby. He'd been there before but it had been years and he'd forgotten how elegant it was.

It pissed him off.

The women could afford it because they were using the blackmail money—*his* money.

Well that was going to change.

A man and a woman stood behind the reception desk. Kong walked over to the woman, put on his friendliest GQ face, and explained that he was there for a meeting with two ladies. He was supposed to meet them in the lobby, but got here late and was afraid they might have gone back to their rooms.

"What are their names?" the woman asked.

Kong wrinkled his forehead.

"That's the thing," he said. "I don't know. I only know what they look like."

He described them.

"That could be Emmanuelle Laurent and her friend," the woman said. "Would you like me to call her room and check?"

Kong nodded.

"You're too nice."

He watched as she pressed the numbers.

718.

No one answered.

"Well, thanks for trying," Kong said. "You're very sweet. I really appreciate your time."

He left.

Outside, it was just as hot as before.

He found a place to sit by the water, a shady spot with an ocean breeze, and contemplated the next move.

His first instinct was to get inside room 718, but he suppressed it. The hotel had too many cameras and security was tight. Making a move there could only lead to disaster. He needed to wait until the women got off-site.

That would take patience.

Usually that was something he didn't have.

But he'd make an exception, just for them.

He called Kam Lee and said, "Did you ever contact that guy?" He didn't need to define that guy. They both understood it was the client, the one who would probably be interested in taking a session all the way.

"I did," she said. "He's interested."

"Will he pay?"

"Yes, but we didn't get into specifics," she said. "He wants to see them first. Why?"

Kong told her.

He might have a lead.

It might be sooner than later.

"I'll tell him," she said. "By the way, for your information, I'm still trembling from that little session you did with me. Next time I want you to stretch me even tighter."

Kong shook his head.

"You don't go any tighter, darling."

47

August 8
Saturday Morning

Michael Chow's girlfriend didn't want to talk at first but then saw something in Emmanuelle's eyes and loosened up. She turned out to be a 20-year-old student at the University of Hong Kong named Sya Bo Lau, majoring in marine biology. She knew Michael was up to something, but didn't know what. He'd been spending a lot of time with people from Paris during the last week. Michael kept telling her he was going to be rich if things went well. It had something to do with finding some kind of treasure.

"Paintings?" Emmanuelle asked.

"Maybe," she said. "I don't know exactly what, but I do know he's real nervous all the time. He's been spying on a man named Guotin Pak."

"Who's Guotin Pak?"

She didn't know.

She sensed he was someone dangerous.

They talked for another ten minutes.

Then Emmanuelle said, "The worst vice is advice but I'm going to give you some anyway because you're such a nice person. Get a new boyfriend and do it quickly. Michael Chow isn't the person you think he is."

She expected the woman to press for specifics but she didn't.

Instead she got a distant look in her eyes.

"I'm going to ask you to do one thing for us," Emmanuelle said. "Don't tell Michael we were here and don't tell him that we talked. It will be better for us that way but more importantly it will be better for you."

Sya Bo nodded.

"Okay."

"I'm serious."

"I know, I said okay."

"Find a reason to break things off," Emmanuelle said. "There's a good man out there somewhere just waiting to meet you. This won't be the end of the world."

The woman's eyes got wet.

Emmanuelle hugged her.

Prarie did too.

Then they got the hell out of there.

At street level, Prarie said, "Do you think she'll listen?"

"If she doesn't, at least we tried."

They researched Guotin Pak on the net and didn't

find much, other than he lived on the south side of the island. "Let's swing by his house and scout it out," Emmanuelle said. "How far of a drive is it"

Prarie shrugged.

"Less than an hour, I guess."

"Good."

The south side of Hong Kong Island, although geographically not far from the city, was a dramatically different world—an island world of beaches and vistas and aqua waters, untamed by man and largely as nature intended it, not totally unspoiled but mostly.

Pak lived in a modest but standalone house on a low bluff, almost close enough for the water to lick if a good-sized storm came in at high tide.

"I'd be nervous living there," Prarie said.

They saw no signs of activity.

They saw no cars.

Emmanuelle tapped her fingers on the dash and said, "We need to get inside and look around."

"You're kidding, right?"

No, she wasn't.

"I'm still freaked out over the key going into Chow's door," Prarie said.

Emmanuelle nodded, understanding.

Then she said, "I'm not talking about right now. We'll come back tonight after dark. Hey, do me a favor, will you? Don't let me forget about that guy who drove by you going the other way after you got released, the guy with the tattoo on his neck. I forgot all about him until just now. We still need to run him down."

"What made you think of him just now?"

"I don't know. The mind's a funny thing."

48

August 8
Saturday Afternoon

Teffinger stood back as Fan Rae knocked on Syling Wu's door. Unlike last time, when no noises came from inside, this time a shuffling vibration resonated and the door opened. A petit young woman wearing a tank top and white panties look surprised to see them. She had sleep in her eyes. The knock must have pulled her out of bed.

She wasn't Syling Wu.

She must be a roommate or a friend.

"Do you speak English?" Fan Rae asked.

The woman shook her head.

Fan Rae looked at Teffinger and said, "Sorry."

Then the two women spoke in Cantonese. After a few moments, the young woman invited them in. The place was small but neat, with a main living area that included the kitchen, a separate bedroom and a bathroom. Two loud air conditioners ran at full speed and managed to keep the place tolerable. Fan Rae must have said something about Teffinger because the woman smiled shyly and then got the coffee pot going.

Teffinger nodded at her and said, "Thanks."

They spent some time there, more than a bit.

Teffinger spent it drinking coffee, looking out the window and wishing he spoke the language. Fan Rae spent it jotting down notes and going through Syling's computer.

When they were finished, Fan Rae said, "She wants to know if she can give you a hug, for trying to help Syling."

Teffinger looked at the woman.

She turned her head, shyly, then walked over and gave Teffinger a hug.

He patted her on the back.

"We'll find her," he said.

Outside, Fan Rae pointed to a no-nonsense eatery across the street and said, "Feed me, cowboy."

"Cowboy?"

"Right."

"You know what a cowboy is?"

"God, Nick, sometimes you act like Hong Kong is on Mars."

He flicked hair out of his face.

"Okay, if you know what a cowboy is, name one."

She hesitated, stumped, then smiled and said, "John Travolta."

He pulled up an image from Pulp Fiction, almost said "No," but then remembered Urban Cowboy, and decided to give it to her.

"Close enough."

They were seated in ten seconds and plates of rice, chicken and vegetables clanged down in from of them three minutes later. Fan Rae told him what all the Cantonese was about across the street. The roommate in the white panties was Tu Lien Lo, who worked as a bartender at Mink on Hollywood Road.

"Mink?"

"Right."

"What's Mink?"

"A hotspot," Fan Rae said. "Think pretty people on leather couches."

Anyway, according to the roommate, Syling Wu worked as a hostess girl, but that was it—she didn't use it as a front for prostitution.

"Syling and her friend, Nuwa Moon, stopped in at Mink for a couple of drinks on Wednesday night before heading to Hei Yewan," Fan Rae said.

"So they were definitely together."

"Right."

"Speaking of Hei Yewan," Fan Rae said, "Tu Lien doesn't know anything about it or the K'ung chia room. She's never been there. G-punk isn't her thing."

Teffinger nodded.

He already figured that out.

"As far as she knows, Syling wasn't into anything weird or in any kind of trouble," Fan Rae said. "She doesn't know anyone with a reason to hurt her. But she knows something's wrong, because it's totally out of character for Syling to just drop off the earth."

Teffinger chewed a piece of chicken.

"So why didn't she report it if she knew something was wrong?"

"Good question," Fan Rae said. "In fact, that's the exact question I asked her."

"And?"

"And, you're very sexy when you eat," she said. "Did anyone ever tell you that?"

Teffinger gave her a sideways glance.

"Be careful," he said, "I'm not above pushing everything off this table and throwing you on top."

She stared into his eyes.

"Yes you are."

"Are what?"

"Above it.

"Not I'm not."

"Okay, then do it," she said.

"You want me to take you, right here right now, on the top of this table?"

"You said you would, so do it."

"I said I could, not would," Teffinger said. "There's a big difference."

"Fine, don't do it if you're afraid," she said. "Anyway, getting back to your question, she didn't report it because a P.I. was already working on the case. He stopped by two days ago and talked to her."

"Who?"

"Some creepy guy," she said. "Her words, not mine—creepy guy. Does that remind you of anyone?"

It did.

It did indeed.

A creepy guy had been in Syling's hostess bar last night asking questions about her.

"Who hired him?" Teffinger asked.

She shrugged.

"We need to find out," Teffinger said. "That's the next step."

"Why? Who cares?"

"We care."

"We do?"

He nodded.

Yes.

They did.

"Why?"

"Because people who hire a P.I. instead of going to the police usually do it because they don't want to be involved with the police," he said. "And the reason they usually don't want to be involved with the police is because they have something to hide."

"So?"

"So, if someone has something to hide, and that person is somehow connected to Syling Wu, I get awful curious as to who it is and what they're hiding."

Fan Rae studied him.

"You scare me sometimes," she said.

"Why?"

"Because you think like them."

"What do you mean—them?"

"You know, the bad guys."

"I don't think like them. I just know how they

think. There's a difference. A big difference."

"Like could and would."

"Exactly."

49

August 8
Saturday Evening

Saturday night was the absolute worst time for Kong to be away from Ra, but he had no choice. Right now he knew where the women were, but if they checked out and disappeared, he would never get this chance again. In the afternoon, he figured out how they got out of the hotel earlier today after he watched the front entrance for an hour—they left by car out of the parking garage. He planted himself by the garage and waited all afternoon. That waiting paid off, because they actually returned in a vehicle—a blue VW Passat.

He wrote down the license plate number.

Then he called Kam Lee at the dungeon and said, "Can I borrow your car?"

"Why?"

He explained.

It was to follow the two women when they left the hotel again.

"Do you just want the car or do you want me to be with you?"

Kong wiped sweat off his forehead.

"It'll be safer for you if you're not around."

"I don't mind," she said.

He considered it. There might be a need for two pairs of eyes. Plus she was good company. He almost said, "Okay," but decided against it, for her sake.

"You'll be involved enough after I get them," he said. "Let's not press our luck. Can you throw some rope in the trunk?"

Half an hour later she pulled up in red Audi, handed him the keys and gave him a long wet kiss before she disappeared. He parked it where he had a good view of the parking garage without being obvious.

Then he waited, for a full hour, followed by a second and a third.

Then, finally, the women pulled out.

He followed them through the Cross Harbour Tunnel, all the way to the south side of Hong Kong Island. Where in the hell were they going?

Traffic thinned.

He dropped back.

The women passed Aberdeen Harbour and Deep Water Bay, then pulled into a parking lot at Repulse Bay.

They got out and took a walk on the beach as the sky changed from late evening to early night. Kong almost made a move, but there were a few too many stragglers around for his taste. Then the women got back in their car, turned on their headlights and headed east towards Tai Tan Bay. Before they got there, though, they turned onto a side road.

Kong turned the headlights off and crept along behind them.

The women made a slow pass by a house on a low bluff.

Fifty meters later, they pulled over and stopped.

Then their taillights went out.

They were sitting there, alone, ripe for the taking.

Half of Kong's brain told him to take them now.

The other half said to hold on for a few minutes and see what they were up to.

50

August 8
Saturday Evening

Saturday night, Prarie and Emmanuelle drove to the south side of the island, bided their time at Repulse Bay until the sky got good and dark, and then made a pass by Guotin Pak's house. No one appeared to be home.

Perfect.

They continued for another fifty meters and killed the engine.

"You still up for this?" Emmanuelle asked.

"Not really."

"Okay, wait here."

"I was kidding."

With knives and flashlights in hand, they doubled back to the house, looked in the windows and saw no signs of life. Just in case someone was inside sleeping, Emmanuelle knocked on the front door.

No response came.

She knocked louder and got more of the same.

The front and back doors were both locked, so they broke a rear window. Emmanuelle crawled through and opened the back door for Prarie.

The main room and the kitchen showed nothing of interest.

But the adjacent room did.

It was an art studio with lots of northern windows. The pungent odor of turpentine hung in the air. A large easel held a panting in progress. Although it was only half finished, Prarie recognized it immediately as she flicked the flashlight over it.

"This is a Renoir," she said. "He's replicating a Renoir. It's not one of the ones at Musee d'Orsay, though."

"Where is it from?"

Prarie didn't know.

"Look at this," she said, flashing her light on a large wooden table. Dozens of detailed photographs of the original painting were carefully laid out. Many of them had yellow post-its with handwritten notes. "I still don't see how he can do it, even with all this reference material. The guy's got some serious talent."

"He better," Emmanuelle said. "He's got five paintings hanging in Musee d'Orsay. He's the only person currently alive who can actually say that."

A faint but definite noise suddenly came from the back of the house, as if someone bumped into something. They looked at each other, then turned off their flashlights.

The room turned blacker than black, so black that

they couldn't even see each other.

They stood perfectly still with pounding blood.

Prarie shifted the knife to her right hand.

In the process, the flashlight dropped to the floor, flicked on and rolled.

The eerie moving beam lit up the silhouette of a man standing in the doorway.

He was big, menacing and stationary, then started towards them.

Emmanuelle shined her light in his eyes and said, "We got knives!"

The man stopped.

No one moved.

No one said anything.

The man carefully bent down and picked the flashlight off the floor and then trained it on them— Emmanuelle first, then Prarie.

"Put them on the floor," he said. "I'm not going to hurt you."

"Bullshit! Step aside and let us out!"

"Just put them down," the man said.

He was on the verge of springing.

The women backed up, one step at a time.

The man followed.

Prarie's heart raced.

They were against the wall now.

"Open a window!" Emmanuelle said.

Prarie felt for a latch but couldn't find one.

"Just kick it out!"

She did.

The glass shattered.

"Get out! I'll hold him off!" Emmanuelle said.

"No! I'm not going to leave you."

"Don't argue! Just do it!"

Prarie pictured going through. There was jagged glass stuck in the bottom of the pane.

She had shorts on.

She'd be cut, probably deep.

Before she could form another thought, the man sprang.

They both slashed at him with their knives.

51

August 8
Saturday Evening

Teffinger learned one thing about Hong Kong nightlife fast, namely that appearance and taste counted. In a city where bottom lines ruled, people dressed to impress. The women were models, the men were clean. Fan Rae hadn't said anything yet about Teffinger's casual attire, but he bought a pricey pair of black pants, and a black shirt, just to keep it that way.

He was nervous about tonight.

He needed to get as much information as he could from the mystery woman without being obvious.

He also needed to do a threesome.

He'd never admit it, but it had him a bit on edge. It would be a new experience. The way he pictured it, he'd kiss one of them, then the other, then feel up one, then the other. How it was supposed to go from there, he didn't have a clue.

He'd just follow their lead.

That's the best he could do.

Fan Rae offered to pick him up at the Fleming, but he wanted to show up at her door and knock on it, more like a date, so that's what he did.

When the door opened, Teffinger wasn't prepared for what he saw.

Fan Rae had taken her beauty to a new level.

She usually wore hardly any makeup, which was a good look for her. But now, with more than usual, her eyes were defined and more mysterious than ever.

Her lips were moist and pink.

She smelled like a flower.

But the best past of all was her dress—expensive, white and short, perfectly framing her ample cleavage.

"You look nice," he said.

"It's called a full hour of work."

"Well, your work worked," he said. "Does that make sense?"

It did.

She hooked her arm through his.

"I'm horny as hell, cowboy," she said. "Consider yourself warned."

They took a cab to the Dragon-I in Central, which turned out to be an already-in-motion DJ-driven party jammed with international jet-setters and the most exclusive local eye-candy, very expensive. A lot of commotion was taking place in a roped-off area by the dance floor. Fan Rae strained to see who is was and shook Teffinger's arm with excitement. "This is so cool. That's Yuki over there."

"Which one?"

"Short black dress."

"The one with the legs?"

"Right."

"Is she someone?"

Yes.

She was, a Canto-pop diva.

"I have all her CDs," Fan Rae said. "I'll play one for you later. God, I can't believe she's actually here in the flesh."

"I take it you're a fan."

"Huge," she said. "We need drinks."

Teffinger handed her a hundred.

"I'm going to run to the restroom," he said. "Get whatever you want and get a beer for me."

Then he disappeared into the crowd.

Five minutes later he returned, holding the hand of a woman in a short black dress, with lots of legs. The look on Fan Rae's face said everything he hoped it would.

"Fan Rae, meet Yuki," he said. "Yuki, Fan Rae."

Yuki laughed at the expression on Fan Rae's face, then kissed her on the mouth and said, "Why don't you and Nick come over and join us?"

"You're kidding, right?"

The woman grabbed Fan Rae's hand and pulled. "Stay close to your man," she said. "A few of the piranhas over there will eat him for breakfast if they get half a chance."

The mystery woman from Hei Yewan—the one who was going to kill d'Asia—showed up half an hour later, already tipsy, and joined the party.

Fan Rae gave her a big hug and said, "Teffinger, Tanna. Tanna, Nick."

The woman looked into Teffinger's eyes.

"You look dangerous," she said. "Are you a bad boy?"

"Why? Do you like bad boys?"

She unbuttoned his shirt and ran a finger down his chest.

"Let's find out," she said.

52

August 8
Saturday Night

A strong moon threw a pale yellow glow over the nightscape. Kong watched from the shadows as the two women walked silently around the perimeter of the house and shined flashlights in the windows.

They were breaking in.

Why?

Were they getting dirt to blackmail some other poor sap?

They were gutsy.

He had to give them that.

Suddenly glass broke.

He smiled.

There they go.

He positioned himself between the house and their car, then searched around until he found a good clubbing stick. He'd knock them both out, then pick up one in each arm and carry them back to his car.

He waited.

Time passed.

Then something bad happened.

Headlights bounced up the road, getting brighter and stronger, heading his way. They came to a stop where Kong's car was parked.

He swallowed.

Police?

They stayed there for some time. Then a car door slammed. The driver must have been out of the car and was now back in. Three seconds later, the headlights moved again. Kong headed farther away from the road and got down on his stomach. Someone could drive by a hundred times and never see him, but the car didn't drive by.

Instead, it stopped twenty meters before it got to the house. The engine shut off. A man got out, a large man, and quietly walked towards the house.

The owner?

The man tiptoed to the front door and tried the doorknob. When it didn't turn, he inserted a key and slowly opened the door. He left it open behind him and walked into the house without turning any lights on.

Kong crept towards the house on cat feet.

Curious.

Excited.

Breathing deeply and silently.

He hoped he didn't have to kill the man.

He really did.

But if it came to it, then it came to it.
He was going to leave with the women. Period.
Nothing in the world was going to stop him.
It was his night.
He owned it.

53

August 8
Saturday Night

Prarie's knife hit something that felt like flesh and, at that exact moment, Emmanuelle screamed. Two seconds later, the side of Prarie's head exploded in colors and pain. She realized that she had been struck by something wooden or metal, something that injured her badly and maybe even killed her. Everything went black before she hit the floor. At some point later she regained consciousness, a foggy eerie consciousness, not fully awake but enough awake to tell that she wasn't dead.

She saw nothing.

She blinked to be sure her eyes were open.

They were.

But the world around her was as black as if she was in a coffin.

She heard nothing.

She moaned to be sure her ears worked.

They did.

She heard that, but nothing else, not a sound.

She had no idea where she was. It felt like a mob of little demons was trying to break out from inside her head by beating on her skull with little hammers.

Let me pass out.

Please.

Please.

She went to put her hands over her ears.

Then something happened.

Something terrible.

Her arms wouldn't move.

She went to stand up.

Her legs wouldn't move.

54

August 8
Saturday Night

Everything went wrong. The mystery woman—Tanna—got pushed aside by Fan Rae, who came over to guard her property. Teffinger spent most of the next two hours sandwiched between Fan Rae and Yuki, getting drunk and being groped. It wasn't a bad place in the universe to be, he had to admit, but it wasn't the one he came here for. He kept an eye on Tanna, waiting for a chance. She was on a couch with her hand in some guy's crotch. Then it was time to leave.

It was threesome time.

Yuki handed him a piece of paper.

"That's my phone number," she said. "It's good for a week or two."

Teffinger shoved it in his pocket.

"Thanks for being so nice to Fan Rae," he said. "You totally made her day."

She rubbed her chest on him and kissed him on

the lips.

"You listen to my CD, okay?"

He nodded.

"Do you do any Beach Boys songs on there?"

She laughed.

"You're too much. Call me."

Ten minutes later they were in a club called M1NT, another high-society Central hotspot, with a Swarovski crystal chandelier that cascaded between floors like a waterfall. The person they came to meet was standing next to a saltwater tank filled with baby sharks.

"That's her," Fan Rae said, pointing.

"The one in the pink and black?"

"Right," she said. "Xiang."

He didn't know exactly what he expected, but it probably wasn't this. The woman had tight pink shorts, incredible creamy thighs, a blue jewel in a very nice bellybutton, and a short black top.

Teffinger swallowed.

She was out of his league.

She might reject him.

The woman spotted them, waved to Fan Rae and then checked Teffinger out as they walked over. She kissed Fan Rae on the mouth and said, "He's just as nice as you said."

Then she kissed him and said, "I'm Xiang."

"You smell like a flower."

"Told you," Fan Rae said. Then to Xiang, "You have a big act to follow. He's been partying with Yuki all night."

The woman was startled.

"Yuki the singer?"

"Right, she's over at the Dragon."

"Well I'll be damned," Xiang said.

They had a couple of drinks and then headed to Fan Rae's.

It turned out that the women already had a plan. They let Teffinger feel up Xiang to his heart's content, to get it out of his system. Then they laid him on his back and said, "Stay just like that, don't move."

He obeyed.

Then they made love to each other.

Slowly.

Erotically.

They did it on top of him, but otherwise ignored him.

It wasn't until they satisfied each other completely that they turned their attention to him.

"We're going to have a contest," Fan Rae said. "We each get to use our tongue and mouth for one minute. Then it's the other person's turn. We can't use our hands or any other part of our body. The one who gives you the ultimate pleasure is the winner."

Teffinger closed his eyes.

"That sounds reasonable."

55

August 8
Saturday Night

As Kong crept closer to the house, the blond woman suddenly busted out of the front door with a knife in her hand and headed right at him. At first he thought she was attacking, but as she got closer it was apparent that she would miss him by three or four steps. She was obviously heading for the car.

Kong positioned himself.

As she went by, he popped up out of the shadows and clubbed her in the chest so hard that she lifted off the ground, landed on her back and didn't move. He didn't know if he'd killed her or not.

He shook her.

She didn't respond.

Then he threw her over his shoulder and trotted towards his car. Her face banged against his back.

Kong didn't care.

Screw her.

He got her in the trunk, hogtied her and then slammed the lid. Now it was time for the other woman. As he headed back towards the house, though, something whizzed past his head, missing him by not by more than a few centimeters. He didn't know if it was a rock or an arrow or what.

Then he saw the source.

It was the man.

He was standing by the front of the house, cocking his arm back. Kong recognized the position.

He ran back to his car, turned it around and floored it.

The back window shattered as sped off.

A death star lodged in the dash.

DAY SEVEN

August 9
Sunday

56

August 9
Sunday Morning

Prarie woke up in a bed. Her wrists were tied together, tightly, with multiple wraps of a thin white rope combined with several hard-pulled knots. Her ankles were similarly bound. Faint background music came from the adjacent room. The pungent odor of turpentine permeated the atmosphere. An air conditioner hummed from somewhere in the house.

She looked around for Emmanuelle.

She wasn't there.

Where was she?

Dead?

The little demons were still inside her head, but not hammering anywhere near as loudly now. She had to relieve herself so badly that she actually thought about doing it right there in the bed.

But the sound or smell might draw attention.

So she fought the pressure and instead surveyed

the rope on her wrists. Then she began working at it with her teeth, quietly, controlling her breathing.

How long would she have before the man checked on her?

Ten minutes?

Ten seconds?

With any luck, he was wrapped up in the painting.

It took forever, but she got the rope off her wrists. Her instinct was to rub the circulation back into her hands, but instead she immediately set to work on the binding lashed around her ankles.

It was actually more difficult than her wrists.

It was harder to reach.

Plus, to pull the knots, she could only use her fingers.

They weren't anywhere near as strong as her teeth.

Finally, though, she got it off.

Her shoes and socks were next to the bed. Should she take the time to put them on? Yes, she had to choice, because otherwise she wouldn't be able to run. She did it as quietly as she could and alternated her attention between the task and the door, which was wide open.

The room had one window.

She unlatched the lock, then slid it up one centimeter at a time, fighting the urge to jerk it up and dive through. As soon as the opening was big enough, she stuck her legs through. She was halfway out when a man appeared in the doorway—a big man, a muscular man, about thirty-five.

Two jagged scars raked down the right side of his face.

He dropped a paintbrush from his right hand and lunged at her.

"You bitch!"

57

August 9
Sunday Morning

Teffinger woke Sunday morning with Fan Rae on one side and Xiang on the other. Both women were naked. Both were beautiful, especially in the soft morning light. Still sexually charged from last night, he almost shook Fan Rae's shoulder to see if she wanted to sneak into the other room. Then he thought better of it, slipped out without waking them and headed outside for a jog.

Hong Kong was still asleep.

It wasn't boiling yet.

He ran for a half hour, still felt good, and kept going. The city was a study in contrasts—yesterday meets tomorrow, east meets west, old meets new, rich meets poor, young meets old, concrete meets water.

Strangely, he felt at home.

He could live here with no problem.

He knew that.

The food was good.

The people were nice.

And, of course, Fan Rae was here.

Fan Rae.

Fan Rae.

Fan Rae.

Who was she, really, deep down?

How did she get such a hold on him?

Or he on her?

When he got back, the women were in the kitchen, wearing T-shirts and equally dripping hair, hinting that they showered together.

Fan Rae tapped her hand on a newspaper and said, "You're famous, cowboy."

The paper had several pictures from last night, namely Yuki partying at the Dragon-i.

She was pressed up against Teffinger with her hand on his ass.

Her tits were almost out of her dress.

"Want's the caption say?" Teffinger asked.

"It says, *Yuki Goes Western.* Everyone in Hong Kong's going to want to know who you are."

Teffinger grunted.

"Well, if they get the answer to that one, I hope they let me know," he said, "because I'm still trying to figure it out myself."

Then something happened, something that made his heart race. He spotted something in the background of the picture, namely the mystery woman—Tanna—sitting on the couch. It wasn't a perfect picture but was a picture nonetheless. Now he had something to show d'Asia.

Yeah, baby.

He slapped Fan Rae on the ass.

"It's going to be a good day," he said.

She slapped his ass back.

"We're getting tattoos today," she said. "Don't forget."

He'd forgotten about that.

"Don't worry, I didn't forget."

Teffinger took a shower, wrapped a towel around his waist and then followed his nose towards the aroma of coffee. Fan Rae poured him a cup and said, "I just got a call from Tu Lien Lo."

Tu Lien Lo.

Tu Lien Lo.

The name was familiar but Teffinger couldn't place it.

"Syling Wu's roommate," Fan Rae added, "the one with the white panties."

He pulled up a visual.

"Right."

Fan Rae punched him on the arm and said, "I knew you'd remember that part. Anyway, she said another P.I. showed up to talk to her."

"Really?"

Fan Rae nodded.

"Someone besides the creepy guy?"

She nodded again.

"A woman, this time."

He was just about to ask *Who?* when his phone rang and the voice of Sydney Heatherwood came through. After catch-up and chitchat she said, "The reason I called is, I gave that videotape to Kwak to enhance, like the chief wanted."

"Right."

"Kwak's been acting funny ever since," she said.

"Acting funny how?"

"I don't know exactly, it's just the way he looks at me," she said.

"Has he said anything?"

"Nothing specific."

"So what are you saying, that he recognized me?"

Yeah.

Maybe.

"He looks torn."

58

August 9
Sunday Morning

Kong wasn't into pain except as a last option. He interrogated the blond woman, Emmanuelle Laurent, briefly last night after he got her secured to an X-frame in Kam Lee's dungeon. She wouldn't talk. Kam Lee took a riding crop off the wall and ran it in a circle around the woman's bellybutton.

"Give me ten minutes with her," she said.

Kong considered it.

He almost consented.

"We'll let her think about it until tomorrow." Then to the bound woman, "That'll be your last chance to do it the easy way. Do you understand?"

Silence.

Defiance.

"That's a promise."

Emmanuelle spent the night on the dungeon floor, inescapably handcuffed to a steel bolt, with the door closed and locked.

Kong went back to Dangerous Lady and fell asleep to the sound of the water lapping against the hull.

That was last night.

When he woke up this morning, the water was calm. He dived in and swam with a strong overhand stroke between the junks and the yachts out into Victoria Harbour and then east along the coast.

His body worked like a machine, a Tarzan machine.

He had lungs to spare, shoulders to spare, arms to spare, kick to spare.

When he got back an hour later, Dangerous Lady had another vessel tied to her—the Predator.

What the hell?

"Jack Poon wants to see you."

"Doesn't that guy ever rest?"

"Be warned, he's in a bad mood."

An hour later, Poon poured two cups of coffee in the penthouse kitchen and handed one to Kong. He took a sip, said "Thanks," and set it down on a newspaper that was sitting on the granite. Poon beat around the bush, feeling Kong out, before he finally got to the point. He had a situation, a very delicate situation, one that required drastic measures and the utmost discretion.

"Are you interested in hearing more?"

Kong shrugged.

"Sure."

Poon studied him and said, "I want someone dead."

Kong didn't flinch.

He expected something like that.

"Who?"

Poon handed him a photograph of a woman, a stunning woman, Kong's equal if there was such a thing.

He tossed the picture on the newspaper, looked into Poon's eyes and noticed for the first time that they had a touch of jaundice.

"What's her name."

"D'Asia."

"D'Asia?"

"Right, D'Asia."

"Nice name," Kong said. "I'm still listening."

They talked money and came to an arrangement.

"Don't look into her eyes," Poon said.

"Why?"

"Because I don't want you falling for her."

Kong laughed.

"Don't worry, that's not going to happen."

He didn't ask Poon why he wanted the woman dead and Poon didn't volunteer. There was, however, one small snag. The woman might be hard to find.

Kong left with a suitcase.

Inside was the picture and cash, a down payment; good faith money, win lose or draw.

He took a glance into the bedroom as they walked

past.

A young woman was sprawled out on the bed, unconscious and naked, the latest and greatest Fion.

Two minutes after the Predator dropped Kong off at Dangerous Lady, his cell rang and Kam Lee said, "Where are you?"

"On my way," he said. "I had an unexpected interruption. How's our friend?"

"Feisty."

Kong chewed on the word.

Feisty.

"Well that's going to change and change fast," he said. "I'm tired of screwing with her."

"You want me to warm her up a little bit before you get here?"

Kong pictured it.

He didn't necessarily like what he saw but needed this part of his life over with.

"Yeah, do it."

59

August 9
Sunday Morning

Something jagged on the windowsill sliced a long gash down Prarie's left arm as she dropped out. She registered the pain and saw the blood but didn't have time for it. She ran, lifting her knees, not looking back and gasping for air.

Shouting came from behind her.

"Get back here, bitch!"

The words were closer than she thought. She tried to go faster but couldn't. Her lungs burned. Her legs hurt. Then suddenly the man was right behind her, breathing heavily, closing in. He must have dived at her, because he got a hand around her ankles and her legs went out from under her. Her chest and face hit the ground, hard, before she could get her arms in front to block. Pain exploded from her nose and blood filled her mouth.

Then the man punched her in the back of the head.

She didn't pass out but everything went foggy and the fight went out of her.

The man lifted her off the ground, threw her over his shoulder and huffed towards the house. She pounded on his back but it was like hitting a boulder. He didn't slow down and didn't even tell her to stop.

She looked around for witnesses.

There were none.

Before she knew it, they were back inside the house.

The door slammed so hard that the windows rattled.

She knew she was about to die.

60

August 9
Sunday Morning

Teffinger didn't know if he would actually go through with the tattoo part of the arrangement, but Fan Rae and Xiang were so excited about it that he couldn't back out. It turned out to be a simple abstract design of three black parallel wavy lines, about two inches long, the brainchild of Fan Rae. They all got them at the same place, namely on the right leg, outside calf.

"Which line am I?" Teffinger asked.

"Which one do you want to be? The one in the middle?"

Teffinger chewed on it.

"Let me be the one on the right."

"Why?"

"Because I don't get to be right that often."

Fan Rae chuckled.

"Okay," she said. "Me and Xiang are the other two."

They dropped Xiang off at her flat, kissed her, and headed over to see Tu Lien Lo, the white panties girl.

She answered the door wearing a white tank top and white panties. She smelled like smoke. Teffinger couldn't resist making a comment.

"You don't like pants that much," he said.

She looked at him, confused.

Then he remembered she couldn't speak English.

Fan Rae translated for him and then translated back. "She says Hong Kong is too hot for pants." The young woman led them to the kitchen counter, poured coffee from a fresh pot and said something to Teffinger as she handed him the cup.

"What'd she say?"

"She said she remembered your addition."

"Tell her fondness, not addiction."

Fan Rae rolled her eyes.

"I'm not going to lie to her, Teffinger."

The women chatted in Cantonese for ten minutes. At one point, Fan Rae showed Tu Lien her tattoo, who then looked at Teffinger shyly, as if in awe.

Then they left.

Outside, Fan Rae handed Teffinger a white business card and said, "That's the P.I. who went to see her."

Teffinger read it.

Brittany So Kwak.

"At first, she didn't want to give her name, other than Brittany," Fan Rae said. "But then Tu Lien told her she wasn't going to talk to her unless she had some identification. That's when she handed over the card."

Teffinger nodded.

"So what did she want to know?"

The answer turned out to be long but simple. She was looking for any information as to where Syling was or who might have taken her.

"The thing that struck Tu Lien as weird was that the P.I. seemed to know somehow that Syling was alive and that someone had taken her. Her words, not mine, taken her."

"How could she possibly know that?"

Fan Rae shrugged.

"She didn't volunteer much," she said. "She mostly asked questions."

Teffinger twisted the card in his fingers.

"I think we need to have a chat with our new friend, Brittany So Kwak."

Fan Rae frowned.

"If she knows something, it's not like she's just going to spit it out. She's a professional."

"Then we need to get some leverage on her."

"How?"

"I don't know," he said. "My job is to think of the problems. Your job is to solve them."

"In that case, I want to switch jobs."

They stopped for lunch and Teffinger took the opportunity to hit the restroom and call the Fleming.

No, no one had left any messages for him or dropped anything off.

Damn it, d'Asia, don't be like this.

Then he called Sydney in Denver.

By the tone of her voice, he'd obviously woken her up. "Sorry to wake you," he said. "I can't even begin to keep the time difference straight."

No problem.

What's up?

"Nothing, really, I just wanted to hear the sound of your voice."

"Bullshit, Teffinger," she said. "Whatever it is, spit it out so I can get back to sleep."

Spit it out.

Right.

Spit it out.

Why did he call her?

He honestly didn't know.

Then he said, "I think I'm in trouble. It's like I'm in a car doing a hundred miles an hour, headed straight for a concrete wall. I can see it ahead of me, plain as day, and I have plenty of time to stop. But instead of putting my foot on the brake, I just keep pushing down harder on the gas. I know I'm going to die, but I just keep going faster."

"Do you want my advice?"

He paused.

Then he said, "No, because I won't take it, and then I'll feel bad."

Silence.

"Nick, you're on the edge."

He knew that.

"But that's where you go when you need to," she said. "That's the difference between you and everyone else in the world. You've always been able to make your way back."

"So what are you saying, No problem?"

No.

She wasn't, not at all.

"What I'm saying is, *Be careful.*"

"Of what?"

"Of yourself."

61

August 9
Sunday Morning

Kam Lee met Kong in the back of the mansion and led him to one of the dungeons
that had a private entrance. Emmanuelle
Laurent was gagged, naked and stretched tight in a
standing spread-eagle position. She didn't look anywhere nearly as defiant as last night.

"I'll take it from here," Kong said.

Kam Lee headed for the door and said over her
shoulder, "Have fun."

Alone with his captive, Kong removed the gag,
then sat on the floor and leaned against the wall.

"It's not too late for you to get out of this alive,"
he said. "But as you can see, I'm out of patience and
out of time. What you do in the next five minutes is
going to determine if things get ugly or if things get
nice. Now I want you to close your eyes and think
about that for a minute."

She stared at him.

"Do it!" he said.

She closed her eyes and kept them closed.

"Have you thought about it?" Kong asked.

She opened her eyes.

"Yes."

"And what's it going to be, ugly or nice?"

"Nice."

Kong nodded.

"Good choice," he said. "Now, I'm going to ask you some questions. You're going to answer each one fully and truthfully. If you lie, even once, the deal's off. Things will get ugly and there won't be any turning back. There will be nothing you can do or say to get you back to where you are right now. I want to be sure you fully understand that. Do you?"

She nodded.

"Say it."

"Yes."

"Yes, what?"

"Yes I understand," she said. "Can I ask one question before we start?"

Kong raised an eyebrow.

Curious.

"Sure."

"Where's my friend?"

Kong nodded, respecting the concern.

"What's your friend's name?"

She hesitated.

Kong gave her a warning glance.

"Prarie Dubois."

"See, that wasn't so hard," Kong said. "Your friend—Prarie Dubois—to the best of my knowledge, never came out of the house last night."

"Is she alive?"

Kong shrugged.

"I don't know," he said. "I didn't stick around to ask questions."

Over the next hour, she told him a story that he could hardly believe, except that it was too strange and too detailed to be fabricated. Her friend, Prarie Dubois, was kidnapped while attending the University of Hong Kong, as leverage to make her father participate in stealing five paintings from Musee d'Orsay in Paris. Emmanuelle was currently working in an unofficial capacity for an insurance company to recover the paintings. Prarie was helping her.

"Why?"

"Lots of reasons," Emmanuelle said. "Primarily to find out who killed her father, but also to get the paintings back where they belong, as a way to restore her father's legacy and reputation."

"Is she going to kill them, when she finds them?"

"Who?"

"The people who killed her father."

"I don't know," Emmanuelle said. "I'm not sure she's capable."

Kong smiled.

"You are though, aren't you?"

She looked away, then locked eyes with him.

"Yes."

"That will be your gift to her for helping you."

"Yes, if she wants."

So why were they on Kong's sailboat?

"We thought that you were the one who picked Prarie up at the club and slipped something into her drink," Emmanuelle said. "That's why we broke into your boat, to try to get more information. That's why we took the computer."

"It wasn't me," Kong said.

"Okay."

"I mean it."

"I believe you."

"No you don't," he said. "But it's true. It wasn't me."

What about the house last night? Why were they there?

That belonged to someone named Guotin Pak.

"Now that we've been inside, we're almost positive he was the one who painted the replicas that ended up in the museum," Emmanuelle said.

Kong cocked his head.

"So he might know where the originals are?"

"Exactly," Emmanuelle said. "At a minimum, he knows who else is involved; and they would know."

Interesting.

Very interesting.

"How much are these paintings worth?"

She shrugged.

"Somewhere upwards of $80 million a piece, in

U.S. dollars."

Kong did a quick conversion to Hong Kong currency.

The number shocked him.

"This is huge," he said.

"Yes it is," Emmanuelle said. "And you can be part of it if you want."

"What does that mean?"

"It means that we'll cut you in," she said. "I have the case on a one-third contingency. I'll give you one-third of my one-third, which is roughly 10 percent. That's $8 million a piece, U.S. dollars—$40 million total, if we get all five."

Kong wrinkled his forehead.

"Don't insult me, I can do the math," he said. "So I get 10 percent, just to let you live?"

Emmanuelle laughed.

"Just to let me live? Hell no, there's a whole lot more to it than that. If we don't find the paintings, no one gets anything."

"So you want my help?"

"Yes."

"How do I know I can trust you?"

"You don't," she said. "Now let me down before I change my mind."

Kong smiled.

"You got some balls, lady."

62

August 9
Sunday Morning

Prarie didn't realize the full extent of Guotin Pak's ugliness until he pulled her off his shoulder and threw her on the bed. That was her first good look at him. He must have gotten the scars at a young age because they hadn't grown with his face. Instead, they sucked his skin in. His eyes were too far apart and his teeth had gaps. He reminded her of a troll. And now he had her—a nice looking woman—in his control.

He glared at her.

Pissed.

He shouted something mean in Cantonese.

She recoiled as far as she could on the bed.

He waited for an answer.

She said in English, "I don't understand."

He switched to English. "What were you two doing in my house?"

"Nothing."

Nothing?

Nothing?

"Did you just say nothing?"

He grabbed her feet, pulled her back into the middle of the bed and flipped her onto her stomach. Then he tied her wrists together behind her back, did the same with her ankles, and then tied her ankles to her wrists, a hogtie position.

"Nothing?" he said. "Talk now, before I lose my patience. What were you two doing in my house?"

"We got lost, and then—"

He slapped her ass.

Then he picked her up, carried her outside where the waves were lapping against the bluff and laid her in a recessed crevice on her stomach, a meter or two above the water, where she couldn't be seen from either side.

He studied her.

"The tide is coming in," he said. "I may or may not come back to see if you're in the mood to talk. If I do, you'd better make the best of it."

Then he was gone.

She was alone.

63

August 9
Sunday Afternoon

Fan Rae's research on Brittany So Kwak re-vealed that the woman was a partner in Phantom, Inc., one of Hong Kong's most reputable and pricy private investigatory firms. "Our office has butted heads with them before," Fan Rae said. "It wasn't pretty," meaning the woman would never reveal who she was working for.

Teffinger studied a printout of the woman's face.

"She's attractive," he said.

"Don't you ever think of anything besides sex?"

Teffinger raised an eyebrow.

"I think of coffee sometimes," he said.

She punched him in the arm.

"Actually, what I'm getting at is that maybe I could find a way to bump into her and buy her a drink," he said.

"You do stuff like that?"

"Ordinarily, no," he said. "But the clock is ticking."

He didn't tell her the rest, namely that he'd been feeling guilty lately. He'd had a couple of abducted-woman cases like this in his day. What happened was always the same, namely, he get obsessed. He put his life on hold. He worked the window of opportunity before it disappeared. But with Syling Wu that obsession hadn't been there. Going out with Fan Rae and Xiang and partying last night was proof evident. He didn't know what the problem was. Maybe it was because she technically wasn't his case. Maybe it was because all this was happening in Hong Kong instead of Denver. Maybe he was just getting jaded. He didn't know why it was. But he did know one thing. He needed to get that obsession back in his life, not in ten minutes, now, this second.

Syling Wu deserved it.

"If there's no front door to Brittany So Kwak, maybe there's a back door," he said. "I don't want to do it though unless you're totally okay with it."

"I don't want you sleeping with her, Nick."

Teffinger grunted.

"I'm not talking about anything even remotely close to that," he said. "All I'm talking about is seeing if I can meet her and then get her to spit something out, before she even knows she's doing it."

Fan Rae studied him.

"It was okay for you to be with Xiang, but that's only because I was there," she said.

They pushed the buzzer for Brittany So Kwak's

flat from the lobby of her apartment building. When she answered, confirming she was there, they said nothing and went across the street to a mom-and-pop eatery to drink coffee.

Their target emerged an hour later, alone.

She wore sandals, white shorts and a light-blue blouse. Her hair was in a ponytail and a large black purse draped over her shoulder.

She walked north towards the harbour.

They followed thirty steps behind.

"This is such a long shot," Fan Rae said.

Teffinger grinned.

"True, but long shots are all you have left to shoot after all your short shots are shot."

She shook her head.

"That doesn't even make sense, Teffinger."

"It's not supposed to."

"Good, because it doesn't," she said. "After all your short shots are shot. What is that supposed to mean?"

Teffinger shrugged.

He didn't know.

"After all your short shots are shot," she said. "Give me a break."

Teffinger laughed.

"You have a very sexy smile," he said. "Did I ever tell you that?"

64

August 9
Sunday Afternoon

Kong was apprehensive about confronting Guotin Pak, not just because the man could throw a death star and was no doubt into Kung Fu or Wushu, but because he was big and strong even without the martial arts training.

Still, the confrontation was necessary.

Pak was the key to everything.

So he headed that way in Kam Lee's car with Emmanuelle riding shotgun.

"Promise me one thing," Emmanuelle said.

"What?"

"If he killed Prarie, I get to be the one to kill him."

"We're going there to interrogate him, not to kill him," Kong said.

"If he killed Prairie, we're going there to do both," she said. "Make no mistake about it."

Kong threw her a sideways glance.

"You remind me of a female me," he said.

"I'm not sure that's a compliment."

"Trust me, it was."

She said nothing and watched the scenery.

"We can't get caught," she said. "I've been hired in an unofficial capacity so I can cut through the red tape. It might be a bit much, though, if they found out I killed someone. They might renege on the fee."

"Then let's not get caught," Kong said. "Tell me about Paris. I've never been there."

"What do you want to know?"

"Tell me about the women," he said. "What are the women like?"

She told him; the women understood their sensuality and weren't embarrassed by it or afraid of it; how they oozed it with their sexy little mouths and their sexy little walks; how every little nook and cranny of the city had a story of lust to tell.

"It's the coolest place on the face of the earth," she said. "Not just because of the sex, but because of the Seine and the architecture and the culture and the cafes and the clubs and the wine and the songs. It's all wrapped up into one big thing."

"I got to go," Kong said.

"When this is all over, you can come and stay with me for a while."

Kong gave her a quick look.

"You mean that?"

She nodded.

"Absolutely," she said. "I'll show you all the secret places."

Kong said nothing.

The woman was just trying to get on his good side.

He knew that.

Still, Paris sounded like fun.

They passed the fishing boats of Aberdeen Bay and then the aqua waters of Repulse Bay. "We're almost there," Kong said.

"So what's the plan?"

"The plan is to take it as it comes."

They made a pass by the house, not slowing down, not being obvious.

The front door was shut and the windows were draped but a vehicle sat in the driveway. Fifty meters later, Emmanuelle's VW Passat appeared on the side of the road exactly where she'd left it. She checked the interior and said, "The keys are still in the ignition but my purse is gone and so is Prarie's. That means he knows my name."

Kong exhaled.

Then he looked around and saw no one.

"Let's get this over with."

They locked the car and headed towards the house on foot.

65

August 9
Sunday Afternoon

Prarie was unconscious when something cold touched her legs—water, just a splash, but enough to make her pull at her bonds with all her might. The tide had reached her. She didn't want to die.

What was the troll doing?

Was he up above, watching, playing a mind game and letting the water lap right up to her mouth before he swooped down and pulled her up?'

Or had he sentenced her to death?

Maybe he'd just silently watch her die from above.

Or maybe he'd taunt her when it started to happen.

She pulled at her bonds.

They didn't budge.

Her skin tore.

She pulled harder.

She didn't want to die, not by drowning, it would take so long.

She'd be so alone.

What would her final thoughts be?

How long would she continue to live after her lungs filled with water?

Would the tide carry her body out to sea?

Would she rot in the sun and be eaten by crabs?

Would the troll pull her dead body into the house and screw her?

It wasn't fair!

She didn't do anything to deserve this.

Help me!

Somebody help me!

Please!

Please!

Please!

66

August 9
Sunday Afternoon

Brittany So Kwak walked all the way to Victoria Harbour and then sat down on a pier. Twenty minutes later a long sleek Predator picked her up and whisked her out to sea.

Fan Rae scribbled down the numbers on the hull.

The vessel was registered to the White Sky Company.

All the stock of that company was owned by one man—Jack Poon.

"Who's Jack Poon?" Teffinger asked.

"He owns half of Hong Kong."

Teffinger grunted.

"Guys like that use P.I.'s all the time," he said. "Our friend could be working on a hundred different things, none of them being Syling Wu."

"True."

Now what?

Teffinger's thought was, Coffee, but when he held

his hand out to see how much his fingers shook, he figured he'd probably had enough for the day.

"Where do you think they're heading?"

"Who?"

"The boat."

Fan Rae retreated in thought. "I'm not a Jack Poon expert, but I've heard his name mentioned in connection with Macau, which is where the casinos are. It wouldn't surprise me if he owned one or two of them. In fact, that would explain the Predator, as a way to shuffle between here and there."

Teffinger raked his hair back with his fingers.

The humidity was so thick that it stayed straight up.

Fan Rae grinned.

"What?"

"Your hair—"

Teffinger pushed it down.

"How far is this Macan place?"

"Not Macan—Macau," Fan Rae said. "Sixty kilometers west, give or take."

"That's a long ways."

"Not in a Predator."

"I mean for us."

Fan Rae cocked her head.

"What are you suggesting, that we go there?"

Teffinger nodded.

"Poon is having a meeting of some sort," he said. "I wouldn't mind know who's going to be there."

"It might only be the P.I.," Fan Rae said.

True.

"And even if other people are going, how would we possibly find out?"

Teffinger looked west, over the water.

"What's the fastest way for us to get there?"

"You're serious," Fan Rae said.

"I am."

They hired a private vessel, a bluewater boat with a deep-V hull and two outboard Yamahas, about 25-feet long, owned and operated by a small man named Chi who couldn't have been a day younger than seventy. When they left Victoria Harbour and entered the South China Sea, the waters got messy and the chop came straight at them.

The boat slammed into the waves.

Bam.

Bam.

Bam.

Then the water got bigger.

Whitecaps came.

The trip only took an hour but Teffinger was two years older, minimum. They gave Chi a good tip for getting them there alive, hopped in a cab and said, "Which one of these places does Jack Poon own?"

"That would be the Cotai Storm."

"Take us there."

On the way, they passed the Venetian Macau, which was almost identical to the Venetian in Las Vegas.

Other equally impressive casinos emerged. The

Casino Lisboa—a festival of domes and curves, something in the nature of a giant lotus flower. The Galaxy Rio Casino—a royal, Italian palace, close to the TurboPier. The Sands Casino—one of the larger structures, with contemporary lines and a smooth skin of yellow glass.

"It's almost like this is a satellite of Vegas," Teffinger said. "Same players."

"It's the only place in China where gambling is legal," Fan Rae said. "It just keeps growing. People are coming from all over Asia."

She had been there twice before.

"Everyone likes Baccarat," she said. "It has the best odds."

"Is that what you play?"

"Me? No, I like craps. You can holler at the craps table."

Five minutes later they were at Cotai Storm Hotel & Casino, a futuristic city from another planet. "I don't think we're in Kansas any more, Dorothy."

Fan Rae smiled.

"Now what?"

Teffinger shrugged.

"All I know is that Jack Poon owns this place and I couldn't even afford to eat diner here."

67

August 9
Sunday Afternoon

Kong and Emmanuelle silently crept to the front door of Guotin Pak's house and turned the doorknob. It was locked. They headed around to the back and found that door beautifully open. They snuck in on cat feet and found themselves in the kitchen. A half-dozen death stars sat on a wooden table next to a razor sharp hatchet. Kong picked up the hatchet and got a feel for its weight.

Faint noises came from the north room.

Kong tiptoed that way.

Emmanuelle followed two steps behind.

The door was half closed.

Kong sprang through with the hatchet cocked, expecting to see his target's startled face turn from an easel. Instead, an iron fist flew through the air from the side and struck him squarely in the face.

He staggered for a second, then dropped to his

knees.

A large body immediately loomed over him.

He braced for the next blow.

Just when it should have landed, the man let out a horrible sound. Kong looked up just in time to see him pull a death star out of his chest. Then Emmanuelle was down there with Kong, prying the hatchet out of his hands.

She raised it to strike Pak.

"I'll do it!" she warned.

Pak slumped to the floor next to Kong.

He put pressure on his chest.

"Where's Prarie?" Emmanuelle said.

"She's not here."

"If you killed her—"

"I didn't kill her."

Kong staggered to his feet, grabbed the hatchet out of Prarie's hand and stood over Pak. "You painted the fakes that went into the museum," he said.

Pak didn't answer.

He ripped open his shirt to check the wound.

It was messy, deep and serious.

"You bitch," he said to Emmanuelle.

"Shut up!" Kong said. He raised the hatchet to strike and said, "Where are the originals?"

"What paintings?"

"Don't play games," Kong said. "Otherwise I'm going to start chopping your fingers off one at a time. Do you think that will help you paint better?"

Pak hesitated, sizing Kong up.

Then he said, "I don't have them."

"I already figured that," Kong said. "Who does have them?"

"I don't know," Pak said. "I just painted the fakes and got paid for them. That was it."

"Got paid by who?"

"I don't know his name," Pak said. "He was just a voice on the phone."

Kong paced, two seconds away from planting the hatchet in the man's skull. Then he made a sour face. "I'm losing my patience," he said. "We're at the point of no return. You need to understand that."

Pak looked at Kong but couldn't focus.

He collapsed onto his back and held the wound.

"I'm bleeding to death," he said. "I'm just an artist. Leave me alone."

Kong stood there, not sure what to do.

Emmanuelle shook his arm.

"He's dying," she said.

"I can see that."

Emmanuelle slapped Pak's face until he focused on her. "Do you have a needle and thread anywhere?"

"Kitchen," he said. "Drawer."

To Kong, "Get it." Then to Pak, "I'm going to stitch you up."

He said nothing.

Then his eyes closed.

68

August 9
Sunday Afternoon

A wave rolled over Prarie's body. She closed her eyes and held her breath until there was no breath left. Then at the absolute last second, the water rolled back and she choked for air. She'd be able to do that two more times maybe three, then the water would be over her for too long, just a second too long but that's all it would take.

She'd breathe in while she was still under.

She'd drown.

She said goodbye to the people she loved.

Then braced for death.

The grim reaper had come for her.

69

August 9
Sunday Afternoon

The Cotai Storm Hotel & Casino had enough glitz and glamour and lights and action to rival the Bellagio or Mandalay Bay or anything Monte Carlo had to offer. Take away the Asian signs and faces, and it might as well have been sitting on Las Vegas Boulevard. Teffinger grabbed Fan Rae's hand, led her to an opulent bar with a octopus tank backdrop, and ordered two Margaritas from a cute woman in skimpy sailor-girl attire. He gave her a healthy tip, looked at his watch and said, "We're supposed to meet Jack Poon in forty-five minutes. Where would that be?"

She thought about it and shrugged.

"I don't know. The penthouse?"

"Right," Teffinger said. "That's what he said. Where's the elevator for that?"

She pointed.

"It's all the way over there," she said, "past the

tigers. The elevator on the right serves the top three floors. There's an operator. Just check in with him and tell him you have an appointment."

"Thanks," Teffinger said. "Can we take our drinks with us?"

"Absolutely."

They headed that way.

Fan Ran linked her arm through his as they walked and said, "You get too much just by using your smile. It's not fair."

"Actually, it only works 80 percent of the time."

"And what do you do the rest of the time?"

"Use my mean look," he said.

"You got one of those?"

He nodded.

"Unfortunately."

They played the pass-line at a party-hardy craps table that had a good view of the elevators and waited. They were down $300 HKD when Brittany So Kwak finally stepped out of the elevator.

A man was with her.

They stepped to the side to finish a conversation.

Teffinger leaned over and whispered in Fan Rae's ear—"Is that Poon?"

"Negative."

After a few moments, the P.I and the man walked away in different directions.

Teffinger and Fan Rae finished their hand.

"You take him," Teffinger said. "I'll take her."

"Where do we hook up?"

Good question.

"Across the street," he said. "The more we're away from the cameras of this place the better."

Teffinger expected the P.I. to get into one of the casino's private limousines for a ride to the Predator. Instead, she sat down at a Baccarat table, laid a handful of bills on the table and got a stack of chips.

Teffinger watched from a distance.

A cocktail girl passed.

He grabbed her arm and said, "What's your name?"

She stared as if trying to place him, then grinned.

"You're the man from the newspaper!" she said. "The one who was partying with Yuki!"

Teffinger nodded.

"Right, what's your name?"

"Yen," she said. "This is so exciting. Is Yuki here? Is she with you?"

"No," Teffinger said. "Not right at the moment. Do you know how to play Baccarat?"

She did.

And told him.

Two minutes later, Teffinger sat down next to Brittany So Kwak and bought as many chips as he could without breaking out the small bills.

The woman looked at him, just for a heartbeat, then turned away.

"How you doing?" he said.

She turned back to him.

"That's not the question," she said.

"So what is the question, then?"

"The question is, *How is Yuki doing?*"

Teffinger smiled.

Then he pulled out his phone, dialed her number and handed it to the woman. "Here, ask her yourself."

70

August 9
Sunday Afternoon

While Emmanuelle cleaned the artist's wound and sewed his chest closed, Kong searched the house. He found the two purses missing from the VW Passat, but didn't find anything to indicate who commissioned Pak to paint the fakes. Maybe the man was telling the truth, namely the person—the he—was just a voice on the phone. The interesting thing was Pak's bank statements which showed five separate cash deposits of $1 million HKD, consistent with Park's story that he got paid and that was the end of his involvement.

It made sense.

What use could he serve, other than as the artist?

On the other hand, would he really get involved in something so big without knowing who the other players were?

And if he did know, he'd have to protect them.

No question.

The stakes were too high.

Stratospheric.

If he gave them up, they'd kill him.

If he even thought about giving them up, they'd kill him.

Pak spent the next two hours slipping in and out of unconsciousness. When he finally got to his feet, he went to the back window and looked out over the sea.

"The tide's going out," he said. "It crested over an hour ago."

"Forget the tide," Emmanuelle said. "Tell me where Prarie is."

Pak got a distant look.

Then led her into the smaller of the two bedrooms.

He pointed to the bed and said, "She was right there, with her hands and feet tied, still sleeping at seven this morning when I started to paint. When I checked up on her at eight, that window that you see open right there was open, and she was gone." He walked them over to the window. "See that blood right there on that little jag of wood that sticks out? My guess is that's hers. She scraped herself when she dropped out. I searched around outside but she was gone."

Emmanuelle wrinkled her forehead.

"If that's true, she would have surfaced by now."

Pak shrugged.

"She probably got scared and headed into the

hills," he said. "You can be up there for hours before you hit a road."

Emmanuelle called the InterContinental.

No one answered the room phone.

She looked at Kong.

"What do we do, search the hills?"

He grunted.

"It'd be a waste of time," he said. "She could be a million different places."

They looked at Pak, searching for lies and finding none.

"If she dies," Emmanuelle said, "you die too. Make no mistake about that."

Pak tensed up with defiance.

"You're the ones who broke into my house, not the other way around," he said. "And you're the ones who swung knives at me. If something happens to her, she brought it on herself. I'm just an artist minding my own business in my own home. She left and she's gone. She's not my problem."

No one said anything.

Then Kong grabbed Emmanuelle's arm and said, "Come on, let's get out of here."

She grabbed the purses.

Kong got in his car and took off.

She followed in the VW.

71

August 9
Sunday Afternoon

When Teffinger showed up across the street two hours later, Fan Rae said, "Where have you been?" He told her—playing Baccarat next to their P.I. friend, Brittany So Kwak. "She gave me her number," he said. "I'm supposed to call her tonight."

"Well aren't you the little Romeo—"

The comment was meant to be light but had an undercurrent.

He wiped sweat off his forehead.

"What'd you get on the guy? Anything?"

"I got enough that you're not going to need that phone number."

He raised an eyebrow.

"Do tell."

"I'll cost you a kiss."

He paid up and said, "Talk."

She told him she followed the man to the Venetian where he checked in under the name Vance Wu.

"How'd you get his name?"

"I got in line right behind him."

"Did he see you?"

"Of course, but I was just one more person checking in. It didn't mean anything."

"So you actually checked in?"

Yes, she did, she didn't have an option not to.

Teffinger scratched his head.

"Why would he check into the Venetian if he's here to see Poon? If he's going to stay in town, why wouldn't he stay at Poon's place?"

"Teffinger, focus," Fan Rae said.

"What does that mean?"

"It means I just told you his name. Vance Wu."

"I know, I heard you."

"And?"

"And what?"

"And, does that ring any bells?"

Teffinger searched his memory.

No.

It didn't.

Was it supposed to?

"Okay, let me give you a hint," Fan Rae said. "What's the name of the missing woman?"

"Syling Wu," Teffinger said. "Okay, I get it, same surname."

Fan Rae nodded.

"That's what I like about you Teffinger," she said. "Nothing escapes that genius mind of yours. Our man, Vance Wu, is Syling Wu's father."

"Are you sure?"

"Yes."

"I already checked it out."

Teffinger raked his hair back with his fingers.

"So Jack Poon and Vance Wu hired a P.I. to find Wu's missing daughter."

"That's what it looks like."

"A P.I. who believes that Syling was taken by someone," Teffinger added. "At least according to the white-panties roommate."

"Right."

"The P.I. must believe that because either Jack Poon or Vance Wu told her."

Fan Rae cocked her head.

"Quite possibly," she said.

"So how did they know?"

"Easy," Fan Rae said.

Teffinger looked at her, confused.

"Easy, meaning what?"

"That'll cost you a kiss," she said.

He paid up, then said, "Talk."

"Easy, because whoever took Syling Wu told either Jack Poon or Vance Wu that he took her," Fan Rae said.

Teffinger pondered it.

"So what are you saying? That she's being held for ransom?"

"That's my theory."

"I'm impressed."

They walked in silence, dealing with the heat and

checking out the scenery.

"The target must be Poon," Teffinger said. "He's the one with the deep pockets, unless there's something to Vance Wu that I don't know about. I wonder if a payoff is set for later today or tonight. Maybe that's why Vance Wu is hanging around town."

72

August 9
Sunday Afternoon

Kong was halfway back to Hong Kong when his phone rang and a female's voice came through. "This is Brittany So Kwak," the woman said. "I believe Jack Poon mentioned me."

"You're the P.I.," Kong said.

"Exactly," she said.

"I'm at your disposal."

"Good, because there's been a development. A man and a woman followed me today from my flat to Macau, where I had a meeting with Poon this afternoon. The man later sat down next to me at a Baccarat table and tried to get in good with me. I played along and gave him my number. Then I coordinated with Poon as to what to do. He wants me to meet the man tonight for a drink and find out what he's up to. He wants you to be in the shadows."

Sure.

No problem.

"Call me with the particulars once you get them," he said.

"We have lots of footage of the two from the casino's surveillance cameras," she said. "Poon's going to email some pictures to you. The guy, by the way, is in today's paper, in the entertainment section. Apparently he was partying with Yuki last night at the Dragon-i."

"Yuki the singer?"

"Right."

"I'm impressed," Kong said. "Who is this guy?"

"His name's Nick Teffinger. Poon doesn't like him."

"That's not healthy."

Kong hung up and switched gears. The woman he was supposed to kill—d'Asia—lived in a fourth-floor flat in a nice apartment building in Causeway Bay, coincidentally less than a thirty-minute walk from his boat.

He headed over, just for grins, and knocked on the woman's door.

If she opened, he was going to punch her in the nose as hard as he could and then snap her neck.

He didn't have time to mess with her.

The real money was in the paintings.

No sounds came from within.

No one answered.

He knocked again, just to be sure.

Same thing.

No response.

Now what?

Suddenly the door across the hall opened, just a touch, and a young girl about ten peeked through the crack. She held a doll in her left hand.

"I'm looking for the woman who lives here," Kong said. "Do you know when she gets home?"

"She hasn't been here for a couple of weeks."

"She hasn't?"

"Uh uh."

"Where's she been?"

The girl opened the door wider and shrugged.

"I don't know," she said. "A lady's been looking for her too."

"Do you know the lady's name?"

No.

She didn't.

"What's your name?" Kong asked.

"Anki Bo Lam."

Kong rubbed her head.

"You're a very pretty girl, Anki Bo Lam," he said. "Your doll's very pretty too. It was nice to talk to you."

Kong walked down the hall.

"My mom has the key to her mailbox," the girl said.

Kong stopped.

Then came back.

"She does?

"Yes."

"Does your mom send her mail to her?"

Anki Bo nodded.

"Do you know where she sends it?"

"No. My mom knows."

"Is your mom home?"

"No."

"Does your mom have it written down, where she sends the mail?"

"Yes," she said. "It's on the refrigerator."

"Can I see it for a minute? What your mom has written down—"

She fetched it for him.

He memorized the address.

Then he handed it back and rubbed her head.

"You're a very nice girl."

73

August 9
Sunday Afternoon

The three additional long breaths that Prarie needed actually carried her through high tide. Each successive breath after that was a little less demanding. Now, two hours later, the water didn't even touch her any longer.

But now she had new demons—the heat, the sun and the incredible screaming of her muscles.

Pak had abandoned her to die.

She knew that.

Then something unexpected happened.

She heard voices up by the house, voices other than Pak's.

"Help me!"

The words came out scratched, weak, the victim of insanely dry vocal cords.

Help me!

Help me!

Please somebody help me!

Then someone said, "Hey! Look down there! There's a woman."

By the time they got to her, she was crying; crying with joy, crying with relief, crying with thanks that she had been strong enough to make it. One set of hands worked at untying her wrists, another worked on her ankles.

Then she was free.

Movement was painful.

The men didn't force her.

They were gentle and flipped her over.

She gasped and recoiled.

They were the men from the warehouse, the friends of the man she shot.

"Well I'll be damned," one of them said. "Look at this."

They carried her up the bluff to the house. Inside, things were worse than she thought. The artist, Guo-tin Pak, was lying face down on the studio floor with a hatchet buried two inches into the back of his skull.

"He didn't have any answers," one of the men said. "You better hope for your sake that you do."

"I don't know anything," she said.

"We'll be the judge of that."

Two minutes later she was in the truck of a car being taken somewhere.

74

August 9
Sunday Afternoon

Suddenly the tires squealed and the vehicle jerked back and forth. Then it crashed into something, hard, and flipped. Prarie's body whipped wildly in the trunk and she covered her head as best she could so her neck didn't snap. The torturous metallic twisting lasted forever and then finally ground to a stop.

A wheel spun, but otherwise everything got quiet.

Prarie moved her limbs.

Her left arm hurt but didn't feel broken.

Voices came, faint but there, belonging to the men, out of the vehicle now and arguing about something. Then they faded into the distance and disappeared.

Time passed.

A vehicle pulled up behind her.

A door opened and then slammed shut.

The car shifted, slightly, as if someone had gotten in.

For what?

To get the keys?

Then the trunk latch released and the lid popped up a couple of inches. Prarie kicked it and it opened all the way. The light was so bright that she could hardly see.

Then someone had their hands on her, pulling her out.

It was Emmanuelle.

"Come on," she said. "We got to get out of here."

75

August 9
Sunday Evening

Fan Rae was down on the casino floor some-where, positioned to follow Vance Wu when and if he appeared. Teffinger called her and said, "I'm going to step into the shower," meaning she wouldn't be able to call him for the next five or ten minutes if Wu appeared.

"Roger that," she said. "Nothing's happening on this end anyway."

"Roger that? Is that what you just said?"

She smiled.

"Yeah."

"Roger that," Teffinger repeated. "You're getting way too into this."

He hung up and checked his watch.

In an hour, he'd meet Brittany So Kwak for their big date. In hindsight, it was probably a waste of time, now that they already knew about Vance Wu's involvement. But this might be his only chance, so what the hell?

He got the shower up to temperature, stepped in and lathered up.

Fan Rae.

Fan Rae.

Fan Rae.

She was a poison.

A sweet poison.

A killer poison.

How did he let himself get this involved with someone like her? A year ago this wouldn't have happened. He was getting weak. He was letting his own personal needs cloud his judgment. He was becoming his own worst enemy. Sydney was right; that's who he needed to be careful of—himself.

Maybe he should end it now.

Maybe he should confront Fan Rae and tell her that he knew about her involvement to kill d'Asia. Maybe he should tell her that he'd turn her in if she didn't drop it.

He stuck his face under the spray.

The water felt good.

It felt clean.

D'Asia was the woman for him, not Fan Rae. He knew it in his brain and he knew it in his heart. He could still feel her from that night back in Denver. If she was around where he could see her and touch her and talk to her, getting the poison out of his life would be easy; no, not easy, but easier.

D'Asia was the antidote.

He got out of the shower, dried his hair with a towel just enough so that it wasn't dripping, and got dressed. Downstairs, he spotted Fan Rae at a craps table, eased in behind her and wrapped his hands around her stomach.

"I've been thinking," he said.

She pressed his hands tighter against her.

"About what?"

"Maybe Syling Wu isn't being held for ransom," he said. "Maybe she's being held for leverage."

"What does that mean?"

"It means that maybe she wasn't taken to force Jack Poon or Vance Wu to pay money. Maybe she was taken to get them to do something."

"Like what?"

"I don't know," he said. "Just roll it around in your brain."

He got four steps away when Fan Rae grabbed his arm and pulled him to the side. "I forgot to tell you—I got a return phone call while you were getting ready for your date," she said.

"My investigation, not my date," he said. "What'd you get?"

"Vance Wu is no ordinary guy," she said. "He's an archeological broker."

Teffinger looked at his watch.

He needed to leave now if he was going to be there on time.

"What's that?"

"He finds buyers for people who are selling expensive, historically unique things—treasures, in effect," she said. "He has a network of contacts that spans the world."

"Sounds like a fun job," Teffinger said. "Travel, exotic ports of call, high stakes, mysterious underground meetings. If you see him tonight, ask him if he wants a partner."

She punched him on the arm.

"Teffinger, you're never serious about anything."

"I'm serious about one thing," he said.

"Oh yeah, what?"

"If you don't know the answer to that then you haven't been paying attention."

He walked away.

Then he heard her shout, "Coffee."

He gave her the thumbs up without turning around.

Fifteen minutes later, Teffinger knocked on Brittany So Kwak's door. She answered wearing a classy gray dress and chic high-heels, neither of which she had when she left the flat this afternoon, meaning she bought them just for this occasion.

She smelled like strawberries and looked dangerous.

For a brief moment, Teffinger pictured her and Fan Rae huddled in a shadowy corner of the night, planning something.

Weird.

Where did that come from?

"I didn't think you'd show," she said.

"Well, I'm glad you were wrong," he said. "So, what's the agenda?"

She shrugged.

"Why don't you take me somewhere and get me drunk?"

Teffinger nodded.

"Sounds reasonable."

76

August 9
Sunday Evening

The Tipsy Typhoon was a bar in the Cotai Storm Hotel & Casino meant to replicate an old wooden pirate ship in the deadly throes of a savage storm, complete with churning waters, ripped sails, lightning arcs and rolling thunder. Jack Poon spontaneously conceived the idea two years ago as he watched a typhoon ravage Thailand on the news. Kong watched his target, Nick Teffinger, take Brittany So Kwak to the darkest corner of the Tipsy Typhoon and fill her with drinks.

Brittany So Kwak looked nice.

Sexy.

Sultry.

Kong liked her.

He didn't like Teffinger though, not a bit, not from the second he laid eyes on him. He wasn't sure he could take the man in a fair fight. Teffinger might have had the same chiseled body as Kong at some point in his life, but didn't now. Still, the man had obvious strength and moved like a cat. Plus he was bigger. More importantly, though, he had a street-fighter look.

Although Kong was ostensibly there for surveillance and protection, he knew otherwise.

Right now, at this second, Jack Poon was watching Teffinger on a flat-screen monitor. There was nothing Kong could see that Poon couldn't. Hell, Poon probably had a microphone planted on the table.

No, Kong wasn't there for surveillance.

He was there for action, if Poon decided he wanted action taken. That, in turn, would depend on what Brittany So Kwak extracted from the man.

Kong's cell phone rand and the voice of Emmanuelle came through. "Where are you?" she asked.

"Macau, on business."

"We had a development," she said. "I got Prarie back."

"How'd you do that?"

"It's a long story," she said. "I want you to talk to her."

"Sure, put her on."

Another female voice came through and asked him a number of questions, none of which seemed particularly relevant to anything. Then Emmanuelle came back on.

"What was that all about?" Kong asked.

"I wanted her to hear your voice," Emmanuelle said. "If you were the person from the club, she'd know it."

Kong grunted.

"Tricky," he said.

"Sorry about that."

"I assume I passed."

"You did," Emmanuelle said. "You're free tomorrow, I hope."

He thought about it.

He needed to kill d'Asia.

He'd get up early and do it in the morning, wrap up by noon.

"As far as I know right now, I should be free in the afternoon," he said.

"Good, we'll hook up then. I have some ideas I'm working on."

77

August 9
Sunday Evening

Prarie got an amazing story from Emmanuelle, about how she got abducted by Kong, taken to a dungeon, and ended up forming a pact with him. Emmanuelle and Kong went to the Pak's house to find Prarie and to interrogate Pak about the paintings. "He said you escaped," Emmanuelle said. "At first it rang true, but then while Kong and I were driving back to the city, I started to have my doubts. I doubled back. Kong never even knew that I did it."

She saw the men from the warehouse throw Prarie in the trunk of a car.

She followed, then got along side and rammed them.

The accident followed.

"I knew you might get killed," Emmanuelle said. "I made a judgment call. It turned out okay but my hands are still shaking."

Prarie retreated in thought.

"So you never went into Pak's house after you doubled back," she said.

Correct.

"They killed him," Prarie said. "One of them buried a hatchet in the back of his head."

"Really? He's dead?"

Prarie nodded.

"They would have killed me too," she said. "Not just because I knew they killed Pak, but because I killed their buddy, what's his name?"

"Pierre Durand."

Right.

Him.

"I can't believe I killed a man and can't even remember his name," Prarie said. "So your judgment call was the right one; they would have killed me for sure The only question is how much they would have tortured me to get me to talk before they did it." She hugged Emmanuelle. "Have I said Thanks yet for saving my life?"

"Actually, no."

Prarie smiled.

"Well don't worry, I will."

Emmanuelle laughed.

"I'll watch for it," she said. Then she got serious. "It's funny how things work. If Pak hadn't put you down on the bluff, you would have been in the house when those guys showed up and started swinging the hatchet. More than likely the heat of that moment would have spilled over to you."

They contemplated it.

Then Emmanuelle said, "Oh my God, I just thought of something."

"What?"

"Well, Pak passed out because of that death star I hit him with," she said. "When he woke up, he looked out the window and said something about the tide cresting more than an hour ago. It didn't mean anything to me at the time. Looking back on it, though, he must have thought you were dead. That's why he didn't tell us where you were, because I had already told him that if you were dead, he would be next."

Prarie shivered.

"This is all too much," she said. "I need sleep."

Emmanuelle did too.

They showered, then fell asleep as soon as their heads dropped.

DAY EIGHT

August 10
Monday

78

August 10
Monday Morning

S ydney woke Teffinger Monday morning with bad news. "The chief wants you back in Denver," she said. "The official reason is that he's stretched the budget as far as he can with this trip of yours. Unofficially, though, if you want my opinion, I think he wants to talk to you about something."

"You mean the videotape," Teffinger said.

"That's my opinion," Sydney said, "but like I said, I could be wrong."

Teffinger looked at Fan Rae, still asleep, so damned gorgeous.

He thought of d'Asia, equally gorgeous.

"Tell the chief I can't leave right now," he said. "Tell him I'm going to pay for this whole trip out of my own pocket. I'm not going to submit any reimbursement requests. So he can relax about the money."

"Nick, you don't have—"

"I'll sell the '67 if I have to," he said. "I have three weeks of vacation coming. Tell the chief I'm taking my vacation time, starting the day I left. As far as the videotape goes, that might become moot anyway."

Silence.

Then, "What does that mean?"

"It means I like Hong Kong," he said.

"You're not coming back?"

"Maybe yes and maybe no," he said. "I have to wait and see how things play out. By the way, don't spread it around. This is just between you and me."

A pause.

"It's that Fan Rae Fan woman," Sydney said. "She has you in her spell."

True.

She did.

But d'Asia did too.

They both did.

"You need to get some distance from that place and clear your head," she said. "You've spent a lot of years and a lot of energy building up your career here in Denver. Do you really want to throw all that away?" She exhaled. "I'm half tempted to fly there and drag you back."

"I just thought of something," he said.

"What?"

"I need coffee."

"God, you're impossible sometimes."

Teffinger found a casino restaurant that served pancakes smothered under strawberries and whipped cream. With a fork in his right hand and a coffee cup in his left, he gave Fan Rae more details about his "date" with Brittany So Kwak last night, where he got nothing out of the woman.

"I came away with the feeling that she really isn't working the Syling Wu case very hard," he said.

Fan Rae cocked her head.

"That doesn't make sense," she said. "If Poon laid his money down, he could walk to the moon on it. You think she'd be billing the hell out of him."

Teffinger grunted.

"That part she's doing," Teffinger said. "I'm not saying she isn't putting in the hours. I'm saying she isn't putting in the creativity."

"Maybe she doesn't have any."

"No, she has it," he said. "She's just not breaking it out."

"How do you know?"

He shrugged and took a long swallow of coffee.

"Just a gut feeling," he said.

Fan Rae got a distant look.

Then she said, "If you're right, maybe Poon hired her to not find anything out."

Huh?

"Maybe she's in a conspiracy with Poon to trick Vance Wu into thinking she's doing an investigation when she really isn't," Fan Rae said.

Teffinger wrinkled his forehead.

"Why would he do that?"

"To protect the person who took Syling Wu," Fan Rae said.

"That's a pretty farfetched theory."

Oh?

Really?

"It's not that farfetched if Poon is actually the one who took Syling Wu," she said. "He'd be smart enough to set up the whole Brittany So Kwak thing as a charade."

"Why would Poon take Syling Wu?"

"I don't know," she said. "Why would anybody take her?"

Teffinger exhaled.

"You're making my brain hurt."

79

August 10
Monday Morning

Aberdeen Harbour on the south side of Hong Kong Island was an endless maze of docks and boats, nestled among clumps and strings of high rise buildings. Fisherman's Village was where the fisherman tied their boats together at the end of the day, free of charge, so long as they had a fisherman's license. They partied there at night and hung fish from their roofs to dry. Just down from that was the Jumbo Floating Restaurant, three stories high and a city block long. Docks were everywhere, housing everything from ancient steel rigs to contemporary state-of-the-art yachts.

Kong had been there many times.

Today, just like every other day, he fell in love with the place all over again.

There was something about the salt, the ruggedness, the luxury and the bustle. Chinamen dressed in traditional garb ferried camera-clicking tourists up and down the waterways in wooden junks that had tire-lined hulls and ragged canopies.

Seagulls flew.

The vessel Kong was looking for turned out to be at the end of a dock.

It was big, steel and old.

Wooden rooms had been added wherever deck space allowed, morphing the once-seagoing lines into something that hardly looked like a boat any longer. Air conditioners stuck out of windows. A large black-and-white dog laid outside on the port walkway. Clothes hung from lines. This is where d'Asia was staying, if the information Kong got from 10-year-old Anki Bo Lam was correct.

He took a seat in the shade, across the waterway, thirty meters off, and watched.

Nothing happened for a long time, then a woman emerged—*D'Asia.*

Kong's pulse raced.

Even at a distance, there was no mistaking the beauty of her face or the lines of her body. No wonder Poon warned him to not look into her eyes. She set a bowl of water next to the dog and then scratched his head as he lapped at it with a long fat tongue.

Then she went back inside.

Kong didn't get it.

What was she doing wasting her life away in a dump like that?

Caring for a sick relative?

Screwing some sailor boy?

Weird.

One thing was clear, though.

It was going to be hard to kill her there.

She was surrounded by activity and eyes.

Plus there was the dog.

Kong was just about to hitch a ride across the harbour, walk down the dock, step aboard and knock on the door, when he spotted a woman thirty or forty meters to his left who appeared to be watching the same boat.

She was positioned where she wouldn't be seen, looking directly at it undistracted by the buzz.

What the hell?

80

August 10
Monday Morning

Monday morning, the Paris P.I. who Emmanuelle hired to get background information on the men from the warehouse called. "I got lots of stuff for you," he said. "And I'll have you know, it wasn't easy. It didn't just drop out of the sky and land on my desk." Ten minutes later, emails with attachments started arriving. The attachments included the contents of the men's computers together with stacks of hard-copy documents that the P.I. took from their houses and then scanned so they could be transmitted electronically.

Emmanuelle and Prarie ordered room service and a pot of coffee, and another pot of coffee, and went through it all.

It was some time before they were done, but they now had a much better picture of their enemy. The men's phone records shows lots of calls to and from a number registered to Gustave Sevenette.

The name didn't mean anything to Prarie but it did to Emmanuelle.

"He bought a beautiful building right on Champs-Elysees just down from the Arc de Triomphe," she said. "He left the first level restaurant intact, gutted the rest of it and turned it into his own private palace. Two years ago he dumped his wife of fifteen years and took up with a 20-year-old Barbie Doll named Darielle Trickett. Does any of this ring a bell?"

No.

It didn't.

"I don't read the papers that much," Prarie said.

"The bottom line is that this guy has a huge bottom line," Emmanuelle said. "Although he's never been formally charged with anything, the word is that none of his money is particularly clean."

"Meaning what?"

"Meaning that every guy in Paris who screws a first-class escort or watches a dirty homegrown DVD is throwing money into Sevenette's wallet," she said. "He's also big into political contributions. He gives favors and gets them."

Okay.

"Here's the kicker, though," Emmanuelle said. "His Barbie Doll girlfriend has an older sister named Lanelle Trickett. She, in turn, is on the board of Musee d'Orsay. The board members, of course, know about the stolen paintings."

Prarie thought about it, then cocked her head.

"So you're saying that Gustave Sevenette learned about the stolen paintings from Barbie Doll who learned about it from her sister, Ms. Board Member."

Emmanuelle nodded.

"The guy we're dealing with, the one at the top of the food chain, is Gustave Sevenette," Emmanuelle said. "He's bankrolling the hunt. The two guys he sent out here from Paris, Nicholas Lefebvre and Pierre Durand, are his henchmen."

"What about the guy who lives here? Michael Chow—"

Emmanuelle shrugged.

"Sevenette needed someone on the team who spoke the language and knew the lay of the land," she said. "Somehow Michael Chow got chosen to fill that role. How people like that find each other is way beyond me."

Prarie stood up and looked out the window.

Victoria Harbour was beautiful, active and vibrant.

Then she turned and said, "So how do we get him off our backs?"

Emmanuelle frowned.

"We can't," she said. "At this point, he'll hunt us to the ends of the earth just to avoid loose ends. In fact, I wouldn't be surprised if he sends someone special just to get that done."

Prarie sat down on the couch.

Then she looked at Emmanuelle and said, "He's the one who killed my father. He either did it himself or gave the orders."

Emmanuelle shrugged.

"Maybe," she said. "Let's check out of this place. We need to go deeper underground."

81

August 10
Monday Morning

Fan Rae got a call to handle a homicide, right now this minute, and couldn't get out of it, so she and Teffinger chartered a boat back to the island. Halfway there, heavy seas and gusty winds set in. The world suddenly turned from strawberry pancakes to a primitive high-stakes battle of man versus nature. They were drenched ten times over by the time they hit dirt but didn't care because they were actually on dirt again, beautiful gorgeous dirt.

Teffinger must have had a look on his face because Fan Rae laughed and said, "Toughen up, cowboy. It was just a little chop."

He flicked hair out of his face.

"You weren't saying that out there."

They swung by her place for dry clothes.

As they were about to leave, Teffinger said, "You know what? I'm going to use the downtime to handle a few things in Denver. Do you mind?"

She didn't, and left.

Teffinger was alone in her flat. He waited for two minutes, just to be sure she didn't forget something and pop back in, and then began the search.

Come on, Tanna.

You're here somewhere.

Make it easy on yourself.

Fan Rae had two computers, a desktop and a laptop. Both were locked with passwords. Teffinger couldn't get into either of them.

All of her handwritten notes were in Cantonese.

He had no idea what they said.

Her bank statements and the like were in both English and Cantonese, but nothing of interest popped out of them. He found no phone bills.

Damn it.

Dead end.

He called Fan Rae, got told that she would be working for a couple of hours at least, and took a cab to the crime scene. It turned out to be a standalone house on a low bluff all the way on the south side of the island, past Repulse Bay.

The body had already been removed but Fan Rae showed him digital pictures.

Someone had buried a hatched in the victim's head.

"Ouch," Teffinger said.

She made a face.

"What?" Teffinger asked.

"That's the same thing I said when I saw him."

Ouch.

"He had a serious chest wound, too," Fan Rae said. "It looked like he got hit with a death star and then someone stitched him up with a regular old needle and thread."

A death star?

What's a death star?

She took him to the kitchen and showed him one. Sitting on the table.

"That could ruin your day," Teffinger said.

"Yes it could."

In the north room was an art studio. A half-finished painting sat on an easel. Next to it was a table filled with detailed photographs of the original. "I've seen this painting before," Teffinger said. "It's a Renoir. Did you measure the size of the canvas?"

No.

She hadn't.

Why?

"I'd just be curious to know if it's the same size as the original," Teffinger said. "Look at these paints. These are all hand-made, not store bought. He was actually replicating the original pigments used by Renoir. That would take a lot of time. You have to do the research first to find out what the original compositions were, then locate the base ingredients, mix them, et cetera. This guy was really going for a first-class replication."

"Why? Is there a market for something like that?"

Teffinger scratched his head.

"I guess so," he said. "The hard part would be aging it. I've heard stories, though, of how it can be done with exposure to bright lights and heat and smoke and stuff like that."

"How do you know so much about art?"

"I do a little painting on the side."

Really?

"I'm in a few galleries," he said. "We'll get on the web later and pull up their sites if you want."

"You're so mysterious," she said. "What else don't I know about you?"

82

August 10
Monday Morning

The woman stalking d'Asia walked across a bridge and then down a crowded promenade next to the water, at the base of the buildings, where the shops and restaurants and bars sat. Kong followed. There was a particularly sexy sway to the woman's walk, a dangerous sway.

She knew how to use her body.

Kong could tell.

Men's heads turned after she passed.

When she disappeared into a noisy eatery, Kong took a seat in the shade and waited. Five minutes later the woman opened the door, stepped outside and looked around. Then she walked in Kong's direction, so close that she would pass within a few steps. He turned his face to avoid eye contact and raised his hand as if to scratch his forehead.

She stopped directly in front of him.

He looked up.

Their eyes locked.

She was nicer than Kong thought, a lot nicer.

He even liked the glasses.

She said, "I ordered for you. Come on before it gets cold."

She turned and headed back inside.

Kong sat there, frozen.

Then he followed.

Inside, she waved to him from a wooden table in the corner. He headed over, found a plate of crab legs, rice and vegetables in front of the empty chair, and sat down.

"I thought that as long as you're stalking me, you might as well be comfortable," she said.

Kong's first instinct was to deny it.

Instead he said, "Thanks."

She held out her hand and said, "My name's Tanna."

Kong shook her hand and said, "Kong."

As soon as the word came out of his mouth he wanted to suck it back in and swallow it.

"Kong," she repeated. "Kong as in Hong Kong or Kong as in King Kong?"

"Take your pick."

She studied him.

"You have qualities of both."

Kong chuckled.

"Oh, yeah? What are my King Kong qualities?"

She cocked her head.

"You have that bad-boy look."

Kong leaned across the table, as if what he had to say was so important that he needed to whisper. She leaned in to meet him halfway, so close that they could almost kiss. "Do you like bad boys?" he asked.

She leaned back and blew him a kiss.

"Sometimes."

"Interesting."

"Isn't it?" She paused, looked him directly in the eyes and said, "I saw you stalking d'Asia."

He kept all expressions off his face.

"Is she a friend of yours?" he asked.

She rolled her eyes at the absurdity of the question.

"Not hardly," she said. "Are you going to kill her?"

Kong's heart raced.

"Why would you ask a question like that?"

"Because she does things that make people want to kill her," she said. "It's just a matter of time."

"How do you know?"

"Just trust me, I do."

After lunch they bought a bottle of white wine, stepped over to a junk and said, "How much do you want for just us two for an hour?"

An elderly Chinese man worked the numbers in his head, then told him.

"Done," Kong said.

They paid him in advance, took seats in the bow and drank from the bottle as the sights rolled by.

"Let's suppose, hypothetically, that you're looking to kill d'Asia," Tanna said. "And let's suppose, hypothetically, that I am too. Wouldn't you think, hypothetically, that we'd have less risk working together?"

Two seagulls flew by.

Close.

Squawking.

Kong looked at her and said, "Why would I bother any more if, hypothetically, you were going to do it anyway?"

"I could ask you the same question," she said. "If, hypothetically, we each waited for the other one to do it, it would never get done."

"That wouldn't be good," Kong said.

"Agreed."

"So, then, have we come to an understanding to work together, hypothetically speaking?"

Kong nodded.

"I think we have."

83

August 10
Monday Morning

Prarie and Emmanuelle checked into a small no-frills hotel in the Shau Kei Wan district, seven kilometers east of Central, under the name Song Chen. The woman behind the desk chuckled at the name and winked. They winked back and paid cash in advance for three nights. Emmanuelle pushed an additional $500 HKD across the counter and said, "If anyone comes looking for two women who look like us, what are you going to say?"

The woman picked up the money and shoved it in her bra.

"I am going to tell them the truth just like I always do," she said. "I never heard of any such people."

Emmanuelle squeezed the woman's hand.

"Thanks," she said. "And be sure to tell us, if anyone comes around."

"I will."

"It's important," Emmanuelle said.

"I understand."

The hotel was on a busy street, above a bar, sandwiched between apartments on either side, with no separation between the buildings. Their room was small and on the fifth floor. The elevator was broken and so was the air conditioner. There were no parking spaces but pubic parking was only a block away.

"I feel better already," Emmanuelle said. "No one would ever look for us here."

"I know I wouldn't," Prarie said.

They got in the VW and headed back to the road where Prarie had been dropped off after initially being held captive for a week. The gas station at the crossroads was right where they left it. A petite man stacking cigarettes watched them from the moment they stepped out of the car.

Emmanuelle got right to the point. "We're looking for a man with a tattoo on his neck," she said.

The man wrinkled an already-wrinkled face.

"Why?"

"It's personal," she said.

He shrugged.

"I've never seen anyone like that."

Emmanuelle exhaled, pulled a bill out of her pocket and held it so the man could see the denomination; $500 HKD.

"Think," she said.

The man retreated in thought.

"Does he drive a small green car?"

"He might."

"There's a man who drives a small green car," he said. "He has a tattoo on his neck. He lives up that way somewhere, but I'm not sure exactly where."

"What's his name?"

"I don't know."

"Describe the car better."

He did.

The back bumper hung at an angle. There was a big dent in the driver's door.

Emmanuelle handed him the bill.

An hour into the search, Prarie said, "There it is!"

She was right too, there it was, lopsided bumper and all, parked next to a standalone structure.

"Is that where you were kept?"

"I never saw the outside," Prarie said. "I'd have to get inside to tell."

Emmanuelle stepped on the gas, pulled to the side of the road two hundred meters later, and killed the engine. Prarie shook her head and said, "If that's his car, then he's home."

"Relax," Emmanuelle said. "We're just going to scout it out and figure out the best way to get in, once the car disappears."

They headed back on foot, hugging the trees.

When they got there, the car was gone.

The structure looked deserted.

"What do you think?" Prarie asked.

Emmanuelle stared at the house. "It could be a trap,' she said. "The guy from the gas station might have tipped him off. If it's not a trap, though, this would be such a sweet opportunity." Suddenly Emmanuelle grabbed Prarie's arm and started running towards the rental.

"What are we doing?"

"You'll see!"

They sped up the road in the direction of the crossroads. The green car came into sight up ahead. It passed the gas station and kept going. They did a 180, parked where they were before and trotted back to the house.

Emmanuelle knocked on the front door.

No one answered.

She tried the knob.

It was locked.

They headed around to the back, found that door equally locked, threw a large rock through a window, and knocked out as much stray glass as they could. Prarie boosted Emmanuelle through.

Ten seconds later Emmanuelle opened the back door.

Prarie stepped inside.

"This might be it," she said.

They headed deeper into the house.

84

August 10
Monday Morning

Fan Rae was just about to wrap up the hatchet in the head crime scene investigation when Teffinger noticed a wooden floor plank under the bed that wasn't flush. When they pushed the bed to the side and investigated further, the wood lifted up easily. In the cavity under the flooring they found a file folder—nothing else, just a single file folder. Inside that file folder were nine photographs; photographs of paintings to be exact; photographs of impressionistic paintings to be even more exact.

Teffinger recognized two of them.

Claude Monet's "Poppies."

Vincent Van Gogh's "Self Portrait."

He didn't recognize the other paintings, per se, but knew who the artists were.

August Renoir.

Edgar Degas.

Edouard Manet.

Each photograph had a date on the back.

"So do you think our dead friend painted these, or do you think they're reference photos of the originals?"

Teffinger shuffled through them.

"They're too small to be reference photos," he said. "He painted them. These are part of his shrine to himself." A pause, then, "Maybe he sold these as originals, then the buyer found out they were fakes and decided that Pak would look better with a hatchet sticking out of the back of his head."

"That's a good theory, actually."

"This is interesting," Teffinger said. "Three of the pictures are of Claude Monet's 'Poppies,' but each one has a different date on the back. Same thing for Van Gogh's 'Self Portrait'—there are three pictures of that painting, but each one has a different date."

Fan Rae studied them.

"Maybe he made a couple of small changes to them and then re-photographed them," she said.

Teffinger looked at "Poppies."

"I don't see any changes," he said. "All three look identical."

"I'll have the lab do a digital conversation and an overlay," Fan Rae said. "If they're different, it won't be hard to tell."

"Let's find out where he banked," Teffinger said. "Maybe he made some deposits that can be traced—a wire transfer or something like that."

Fan Rae smiled.

"You're pretty sexy when you think," she said.

"Did anyone ever tell you that?"

Teffinger grunted.

"As a matter of fact, Sydney Heatherwood said that to me once," he said. "She also added, Good thing it doesn't happen that often."

"That is so freaky."

"Why?"

"Because I was just about to say that same thing."

"Great, just what I need in my life, two Sydneys."

"I want to meet her," Fan Rae said.

"No way," Teffinger said. "She has too many stories about me."

"Any bedroom stories?"

Teffinger shook his head.

"She's my partner," he said. "Even I have a few boundaries." He cocked his head and added, "I did bounce a quarter off her ass once, though."

"Tell me about it," Fan Rae said. "But not now, the next time we're drunk.'

They learned a lot over the next few hours. The five paintings depicted in the photographs were all from the same place, namely Musee d'Orsay in Paris, France. Teffinger was right about the other three artists.

The Renoir was called "Nude in the Sunlight."

The Degas was "Absinthe."

The Manet was "At the Beach."

The interesting thing, though, was that the three photographs of Claude Monet's "Poppies" were all slightly different paintings, rather than refinements or modifications of the same one

"He painted that one three different times," Teffinger said. "I wonder why."

"Maybe he didn't like the way the first two came out," Fan Rae said. "It took him three tries to get it the way he wanted it."

Teffinger shrugged.

Maybe.

But the first two looked pretty good to him.

The same was true of Van Gogh's "Self Portrait." It got painted three separate times.

The other interesting thing related to Pak's bank account. He deposited $1,000,000 HKD on five separate occasions, cash each time.

"He sold them to someone for a million each," Fan Rae said.

Teffinger nodded.

That was true.

"One thing baffles me," Fan Rae said. "If he painted nine paintings and sold five, what happened to the other four?"

Teffinger shrugged. He didn't know.

"The other thing that baffles me is—"

"Wait a minute, cowgirl."

"What?"

"You said *One thing baffles me*," Teffinger said. "Emphasis on the One. Now you're adding a second thing."

"I can't add to the baffle list?"

"Baffle lists are set in stone," he said. "You can't mess with baffle lists."

She punched him on the arm.

"Okay, let me put it like this," she said. "In addition to the *One thing that baffles me*, there's something that interests me too."

Teffinger nodded.

"Better," he said.

"And that is, who would be crazy enough to pay $1,000,000 for these replicas? There's no way he could sell them as originals. Anyone with an Internet connection can find out in two minutes that the originals are in Musee d'Orsay."

Teffinger shrugged.

"It is baffling," he said.

"And interesting."

85

August 10
Monday Morning

A man named Dewel Ho Shek owned the steel vessel in Aberdeen Harbour where d'Asia was staying. He went by the name Billy— Billy Shek—but only among friends. In the photography world he still used his legal name, probably because it had a more professional ring to it.

"Billy," Kong said. "I saw a spaghetti western about Billy the Kid when I was about ten. That's the only Billy I've ever known."

"Well now you know two," Tanna said.

"What's he like?"

"He's big."

"That's not good."

No, it wasn't.

"D'Asia hardly ever leaves the boat," she said. "When she does, it's usually just a quick trip on foot up to the stores. Billy gets home at the same time every day, about five o'clock. They hang out inside until after dark. Then they come out on deck and drink wine."

"So they're lovers?"

Tanna shook her head.

"No, they're just friends," she said. "I'm sure he'd like it to be more, but she's way out of his league."

Kong spotted a rock and threw it at duck.

He missed, but got close enough to scare the bird into the air.

"You've done your homework," he said.

"I've been at this a while," she said. "I'm ready for it to end. Here's my plan. I'm going to find a way to make a move on Billy and get him to take me out. That will leave d'Asia alone, after dark. You swoop in and kill her."

Kong chewed on it.

"Works for me," he said. "We'll do it tonight. If you can't lure him away, we'll both swoop in. I'll take care of him and you can take care of her."

Okay.

Fine.

"Either way, it's done and over tonight."

86

August 10
Monday Morning

Prarie and Emmanuelle headed deeper into the tattoo man's house. In the basement, at the end of a large room, they spotted a solid steel door. They opened it to find a windowless room with a bed and a bathroom.

"This is it!" Prarie said.

"Are you sure?"

"You got to be kidding," Prarie said. "I know every square inch of this place. Look at me, I'm shaking." She held her hand out to prove it. Sure enough, it trembled.

Emmanuelle got a strange look on her face.

Prarie sensed trouble, then she understood.

Someone was in the house, upstairs.

There was no way to get to the outside from this level. The only way out was to go up.

"What do we do?" Prarie whispered.

"It might have been a trap after all. If it's not,

he's going to spot the broken window any second," Emmanuelle said. "We need to get out of here now before it's too late."

She headed for the stairs. Prarie tried to follow but she couldn't breathe and sank to the floor.

87

August 10
Monday Afternoon

Teffinger called The Fleming to see if anyone left a message. No one had. He couldn't justify the expense any longer and checked out as long as he was on the line. When he hung up, Fan Rae wanted to go back to Guotin Pak's house and have another look around.

"Why?"

"Because there's too much going on," Fan Rae said. "We got blood on the windowsill, as if someone crawled through it and got scraped on the way down. We got lengths of rope lying around, as if someone had been tied up. We got the victim injured with a death star, then sewed up, then snagged in the head with a hatchet. There's a story that connects it all and I want to know what it is." She patted Teffinger on the knee. "You want to come with me?"

Teffinger cocked his head.

The Pak murder was interesting.

It was fresh.

He didn't have a dog in that fight, however.

He needed to stick with Syling Wu.

On the other hand, he had no idea what to do next in that case.

"I'll tag along," he said.

At Pak's, they parked in the driveway, unlocked the door and stepped inside. Fan Rae said, "I'm going to use the facilities," and headed that way. Teffinger thought he heard something in the studio.

Weird.

He listened harder.

Silence.

When he walked into the room, a fist came out of nowhere and smashed him on the side of the head.

Hard.

Serious.

He tried to stay on his feet but staggered and then dropped to the floor. His eyes focused just long enough to see a man dive headfirst through the back window, right through the glass.

Then everything went fuzzy.

"Nick!"

Suddenly Fan Rae was there with him, pressing something cold and wet onto the side of his head, stopping the bleeding.

"Did you see who did it?" she asked.

"Just a bit," Teffinger said. "I think it was Vance Wu but I'm not positive."

"Vance Wu?"

"Right."

"Vance Wu from the casino?"

"Yes."

"Are you sure?"

"No."

"What would he be doing here?" Fan Rae asked.

Teffinger shrugged.

"I don't know but I'll tell you one thing," he said. "Whoever it was, I'm impressed. I've seen guys jump through windows on TV a million times, but that's with safety glass and mats. This guy did it for real. You got to be a little bit nuts to do it for real. If it was me, I would have taken the extra half second to go through the front door. I wonder if he cut himself."

He staggered to his feet, tested his balance and eased his way over to the window.

The glass was shattered.

They saw no blood, not a drop.

"Now I'm even more impressed," Teffinger said. He felt something warm on his neck and touched it.

"Nick, sit down. You're bleeding all over the place."

Fan Rae's phone rang. She spoke in Cantonese and increasingly wrinkled her forehead as she talked. Two minutes later she hung up and said, "I'm going to have to bail on you for a few hours tonight."

Why?

What's up?

"I need to help someone with a project," she said.

Teffinger opened his mouth to ask another question, then he paused.

He suddenly realized what was going on.

Fan Rae and Tanna were going to kill d'Asia tonight.

He looked at her, searching for something on her face to tell him he was wrong, but her face was stone, cold stone, hard stone.

"What's that look for?" she asked.

"I have a look?"

Yes.

He did.

"You're looking at me with a look."

"I guess it's just that I pictured us together tonight," he said.

She kissed him.

"I won't be gone for long," she said. "To make up for it, when I come back I'll be your sex slave."

88

August 10
Monday Afternoon

When Poon called Kong shortly after lunch and wanted to know what Kong was doing, he told him he was smack in the middle of planning the d'Asia project, which was going to go down tonight. Kong flirted briefly with the thought of telling Poon about Tanna, but didn't see an upside to it. "Do you want to make some money this afternoon equal to the d'Asia project?" Poon asked.

"Are you serious?"

"Yes. Dead."

"I'll have you back in plenty of time for tonight," Poon said.

A half hour later, the Predator picked Kong up at Aberdeen Harbour and whisked him to Macau. There, he was met at the dock by Jack Poon and Vance Wu.

"Do you know how to drive a boat like this?"

Poon asked.

"You mean twin screws? Sure, no problem."

"Good. We're going to go on a little treasure hunt for our eyes only."

"What kind of treasure hunt?"

"The kind you won't even believe."

Interesting.

They lashed a rubber dinghy to the swim platform and headed southeast into the South China Sea. Twenty kilometers later they hit the Dongoo Dao islands. Poon directed them to the smaller island, to the east, which was less than a half kilometer around. On the south side sat a sandy beach.

Deserted.

"I own this island," Poon said.

"Nice."

"Not nice, paradise," Poon said. "I bring women here sometimes."

"Nice work if you can get it," Kong said.

They anchored the Predator in fifteen feet of clear aqua water, threw a shovel into the dinghy and rowed ashore. When they got there, Poon pulled a gun from out of nowhere and pointed it at Wu.

He made a mark in the sand with his foot, not more than a few meters from the edge of the water, and told Kong to start digging.

Kong was pretty sure what Poon had planned but he didn't know why nor did he perceive Poon to be in the mood to answer questions, so he picked up the shovel and dug, and didn't stop until Poon told him to.

Then Poon said, "Put him in."

Kong pushed Wu in.

"Fill it up but let his head stick out."

Kong did it.

Within five minutes, Vance Wu was buried up to his neck in the sand.

Poon squatted down and looked Wu in the eyes.

"I saw this once in an old pirate movie and promised myself I'd do it to someone some day," he said. "Apparently, you're the someone and today is the day."

Wu wasn't impressed.

"I heard about your scare club," he said. "This isn't going to work. You're going to have to find another sucker."

Poon looked out at the sea.

"The tide's coming in," he said.

89

August 10
Monday Afternoon

The footsteps coming from upstairs suddenly stopped. Prarie pictured the man with the tattoo staring at the broken window, stopping in his tracks, and listening for someone in the house. She pictured him tiptoeing to get a knife or a gun or a hammer. Instead, the front door opened and then closed. A few seconds later, a car fired up outside and drove away.

They tiptoed up the stairs, looked around, saw no one and got the hell out of there.

When they passed the gas station at the crossroads, the small green car was next to a pump. A strong man with a wild tattoo on his neck was filling the tank. He fixated on the women as they drove past.

"He recognized me," Prarie said.

Emmanuelle pushed harder into the pedal.

"No way," she said. "Not with your new hair."

"No, he did," Prarie said. "I saw it in his eyes. He

recognized me but just couldn't place it. Once he finds out the house was broken into, he'll figure it out."

The tires squealed.

The car drifted over the line.

Emmanuelle brought it back and said, "It doesn't matter. He'll never find us."

Prarie grunted.

"He'll be calling every hotel in Hong Kong within the next half hour," she said.

"Relax," Emmanuelle said. "You worry too much."

On the drive back, Emmanuelle made a phone call to her P.I. friend in Paris and gave him a new assignment. He said, "I'm on it," and called back in twenty minutes. "Okay, that house is titled to a man named Dick Jin Lin. Just for grins, I ran a preliminary background check on him. Stay away from him."

"Why?"

"You don't want to know."

Yes she did.

So he told her.

"Do me a favor and dig deeper," she said. "I want to know who his friends are."

"How am I supposed to find that out from Paris?"

"I don't know. I only know that I need you to."

When they got back to the hotel, the elderly woman at the reception desk frowned when she saw them.

They sensed trouble.

"What's wrong?" Emmanuelle asked.

"You were right," the woman said. "Someone came looking for you."

"Who?"

The woman handed her a black and white print-out of a man's face. "I printed this off our security tape for you," she said.

Emmanuelle studied the face.

Prarie did too.

It was a man in his mid-thirties, good looking, with a square chin, jet-setter eyes and a refined-slash-rugged look. He'd be right at home dining at the finest restaurant or trekking through the wettest rainforest. He looked like a man who knew what he wanted in life and had figured out how to manipulate the world to get it.

"Is that Gustave Sevenette?" Prarie asked.

Emmanuelle shook her head.

"No."

"Who is it?"

"I don't know," Emmanuelle said. Then to the elderly woman, "Did he speak French?"

"He spoke English but had a French accent."

Emmanuelle retreated in thought.

Then she said, "Is there a back way out of here?"

The woman pointed. "Down that hall until it ends, then to the right until it ends, then to the left. You'll be in an alley."

Emmanuelle gave the woman another bill, $500 HKD.

"You did good, thank you." Then to Prarie, "You

go to the alley. I'm going to get our stuff and then I'll meet you there."

"I'll come with you."

"It's better if you don't, in case he's up there."

90

August 10
Monday Afternoon

Tonight was the night. Fan Rae and Tanna would set out into the darkness to kill d'Asia. All afternoon, Teffinger kept a normal face and spoke normal words, but it was a major effort. Everything he had built with Fan Rae would shatter and collapse in matter of hours.

She was a bad girl, a bad girl who made him love her.

That's right, he loved her.

He probably still would, even when everything was over.

God, what a mess.

Late afternoon, he made an excuse to get out for an hour, rented a blue Honda Accord, and parked it where he'd be able to follow Fan Rae when she left tonight.

He thought about confronting her but knew only bad could come of it.

She'd deny everything.

She'd abort tonight.

Then she'd kill d'Asia later when he wasn't around.

No, words wouldn't work.

He needed to catch her in the act.

He needed to stop her in the act, to be more precise.

That was the only way to save d'Asia.

And that's what he came here for.

His phone rang. The incoming number belonged to Sydney Heatherwood.

He didn't answer.

She was probably calling with bad news.

He didn't need it, not right now.

91

August 10
Monday Afternoon

Jack Poon sat down in the sand next to Vance Wu's face, patted the man on the top of his head, and stretched his legs out. A cool breeze rolled off the ocean. Three seagulls flew over and landed ten steps away. "Humans mean food," Poon told Kong. "That's why they just came over here, the birds. Every living thing on the planet is looking to survive." He chuckled. "Not me, though. I'm way past surviving. I have enough money to survive a thousand lifetimes. Now I'm a man of taste and culture. But that's not without its own set of problems. Taste and culture can get you in trouble. Do you want to know how?"

Kong nodded, curious.

"Sure," he said.

Poon looked at him.

"You're going to go far in my organization," Poon said. "You have the qualities I've been looking for.

You're moving up, even as we sit here, you're moving up. Is that what you want?"

Yes, it was.

"Good," Poon said. "Anyway, getting back to taste and culture, a man approached me a while back, a man by the name of Guotin Pak. Have you ever heard of him?"

No, Kong hadn't.

"I hadn't either at the time," Poon said. "He said he was an artist and had a proposition for me. He said he could paint exact replicas of some of the old impressionistic paintings in Musee d'Orsay in Paris, France. Have you ever heard of that museum?"

Yes, he had.

"Everyone has," Kong said.

"That's what I like about you Kong," Poon said. "You're got education. Anyway, he said he could paint these replicas and that they could be hung in place of the originals and no one would know the difference, if someone could figure out how to get the originals out and get them in. I said, That's interesting, and that was basically the end of it." Poon smiled. "That brings us to that taste and culture problem I was telling you about. I started to think how cool it would be to own a few priceless pieces from the old masters. You see, that's the kind of thing you can't buy. And I came up with a plan to get the originals out and the replicas in."

Kong was stunned.

"You did?"

Poon nodded.

"It was pretty simple, really," he said. "One thing you'll learn as time goes on, Kong, is how to delegate. In this case, I delegated the problem to a man named Jean-Didier Dubois, who worked in the restoration department of the museum. His daughter—a young lady named Prarie Dubois—was attending the University of Hong Kong, which was a coincidence but not really relevant. She could have been going to school in Rome or London and it wouldn't have made any difference. Anyway, to get to the point, I had her abducted. I told her father, Jean-Didier Dubois, that he'd get her back when and if he switched the paintings. You see, he was in a position to do it because he had access to everything in the museum. He thought about it and told me he wouldn't be able to do it without the cooperation of the security department. The head of that department was a man by the name of Yves Blanc. Luckily, he also had a daughter, a young lady by the name of Dominique Blanc. We didn't actually have to kidnap her. Just the threat of doing that was enough to get Yves on board. The two of them, meaning John-Didier and Yves, then figured out how to get the exchanges done."

Poon paused.

He picked up a handful of sand.

It fell through his fingers onto the top of Vance Wu's head.

"Vance, I'm telling the truth about all this, right?"

Silence.

Poon laughed.

Then to Kong, "You'll have to excuse Vance, it appears he's not in a very good mood right now. We made the exchanges, five in all, over a week's period. I now had five original priceless paintings in my possession."

Poon sighed.

"Art is nice, but money is nicer," he said. "By that time, I had already decided to sell them once I got them. They were worth roughly $80 million each, in U.S. dollars. Pak had a friend—namely this man right here, Vance Wu—who had spent his life brokering rare archeological treasures. He had the contacts in place to sell the paintings on the black market. I decided to use him for the sale. Are you following me so far?"

"Yes."

The seagulls flew off.

"That's when Vance here, and his artist friend Guotin Pak, came up with a brilliant twist," Poon said. "Pak would paint a second fake of one of the paintings. The original painting would be shown to the buyer—who, of course, would have someone there to confirm that it was in fact an original. After it got confirmed, Vance would switch the two, and the buyer would leave with a fake. Then he'd bring the original back to me together with the purchase money."

Poon nodded at Vance.

"That took guts," Poon said. "Vance was hanging out. If he got caught, he would have been killed on the spot. But that's what we did. For one of the original paintings, namely Van Gogh's 'Self Portrait,' Pak painted a second fake. The original was shown to a potential buyer in Paris by the name of Jacques Girard. He brought two people with him who confirmed that the original was in fact the original. The painting was out of the frame but still on the stretchers at that point. Vance put it in the adjacent room, with a bodyguard, while he counted the purchase money. The bodyguard brought the fake out when the transaction was done and that's what the buyer left with."

Kong nodded.

"Tricky," he said.

"Tricky and lucrative," Poon said. "Pak, of course, got another million for painting a second fake. Vance, for his part, got a 10% bonus, on top of his 10% commission, meaning 20%, which came to $16 million, U.S. dollars. I then got the balance of the sales proceeds—roughly $64 million—and still had the original painting. No one even knew who I was. That worked so well that we also did it a second time, with Claude Monet's 'Poppies.' A fake of that painting got sold to a man named Sam Yamid in Cairo, Egypt."

"So it all worked out well," Kong said.

Poon nodded.

"For the other three, we simply sold the originals," Poon said. "We didn't want to press our luck." He smiled. "You can't get greedy, Kong. Always remember that. Greed will kill you."

"Right."

"I'm serious," Poon said.

"I understand."

"Anyway, to continue," Poon said, "Vance here had to go underground. Obviously, sooner or later, these two buyers would figure out what happened. Vince couldn't be around at that point in time."

"Understood."

"But no biggie," Poon said. "He had enough money to live on comfortably for the rest of his life, right Vance?"

"I don't understand what's going on," Vance said.

Poon patted him on the head.

"You will in a minute," he said. "What happened next is unfortunate," Poon said. "The buyer in Paris, Jacques Girard, figured out he'd been duped. He went looking for Vance—at least I assume he did, that's what I would have done—but couldn't find him. So what he did was take Vance's daughter, a young lady by the name of Syling Wu. Then he left a phone message for Vance to call him. Vance suspected something like that happened when could no longer get in touch with Syling. He called Jacques Girard, to feel him out. That was an ugly conversation. Mr. Girard not only confirmed that he had Syling, but also reported that he had killed Syling's friend, as an example of how serious he was. The friend was named Nuwa Moon. Mr. Girard said he carved a K'ung chia symbol into the girl's stomach and slit her throat. He said that the same thing would happen to Syling unless Vance produced the original painting."

"Wow," Kong said.

"Things can get dicey when the stakes get high," Poon said.

"Apparently."

"Extreme measures follow big money around like parasites," Poon said. "That's why I need someone like you in my organization. I guess I should ask you at this point if you're still interested in the job, now that you know some of the stuff that's going on."

Kong flicked his hair.

"No problem."

Good.

Very good.

"We're getting near the end of the story," Poon said. "Vance came to me and told me how Syling had been abducted. He wanted me to give him the original panting back so he could give it to Girard and get Syling back. I told him I had already sold it." Then to Vance, "By the way, Vance, that was a lie. I had it at that point in time and still do. I just didn't want to give it up." Back to Kong, "What I did do, though was hire a P.I. by the name of Brittany So Kwak to see if she could figure out where Syling was being kept, so I could launch a rescue mission. So far, however, she hasn't come up with anything."

"Ouch," Kong said.

Right.

Ouch.

Poor Syling.

"Are you ready for the end of the story?" Poon

asked.

Kong nodded.

"This is fascinating," he said.

"Wait until you hear the last part," Poon said. "It's going to interest Vance, too. Here it is. All this activity got me refocused on the two original paintings that I had in my possession. They're hanging in my penthouse, by the way. Just for grins, I had a third party take a look at them, just to confirm that they are the originals. The answer surprised me."

Vance squirmed in the sand.

Poon chuckled.

"To my surprise, they turned out to be fakes," Poon said. "Both of them. Of course, I started to wonder how that could possibly be true. Then I figured it out. Vance and his little buddy, Guotin Pak, came up with yet another new twist, only this one they didn't share with me. Their plan was simple and brilliant. Pak would actually paint a third fake of each of these two paintings. Then, when the originals were supposed to come back to me, it would actually be two fakes coming back."

Poon looked at Vance.

"So tell me Vance, did I get it right?"

The man's face contorted in terror.

"I still have one of the originals," Vance said. "It's all yours. I'll get it for you."

"Where's the other original?"

"Pak has it."

"So that was your conspiracy with him then?"

Poon asked. "That you would each keep one?"

Silence.

Then Vance said, "Yes, but it was Pak's idea, not mine. In fact, the more I think about it, I think that was Pak's plan all along from the very beginning—not to just get paid to paint a few fakes, but to actually end up with an original."

Poon considered it.

"Wow, I never saw that coming, but it makes sense," he said. "If that actually is the case, the man is brilliant. But back to you, my friend. Which original did you keep?"

"The Van Gogh."

"The 'Self Portrait?'"

"Yes."

"Where is it?"

"If I tell you, will you let me go?"

"Of course," Poon said. "This is all just business. You'll need to return all the money you got from me too."

"Of course."

"Do you still have it?"

"Most of it."

"Good. So where's the original Van Gogh?"

Vance told him.

It was in a storage locker.

The key was in Vance's desk.

"Good," Poon said. "See how easy that was?"

"So let me out now," Vance said.

"Of course," he said. "That was the deal."

92

August 10
Monday Afternoon

Poon stood up.

He shoveled sand away from Vance's head.

Then he paused.

"Wait, there is one more piece of business."

Vance sensed danger.

"What?"

"You had the original painting when Jacques Girard asked for it," Poon said. "You could have used it to free Syling. But you didn't."

Silence.

"Instead, you kept it, and tried to see if I, or a P.I. hired by me, could get you out of your mess," Poon said. "You could have freed your daughter the whole time but didn't. What kind of father does a thing like that?"

Poon looked at Kong.

"That's the greed part I was talking about before. Remember when I said to not be greedy? That greed will kill you?"

Kong nodded.

He remembered.

Poon squatted down and looked Vance Wu in the eyes. "You're not going to stay here because of what you did to me. That I could forgive. In fact, I admire your cunning. But you are going to stay here because of what you did to your daughter. A man who does something like that to his own flesh and blood doesn't deserve to live."

He kicked sand in the man's face.

Then he said to Kong, "Let's go."

They rowed back to the Predator, raised the anchor and took off.

In Macau, Kong called Emmanuelle the first chance he got. "Guotin Pak has one of the original paintings," he said. "He has the original Claude Monet, the one called 'Poppies.'"

"How do you know?"

"It's a long story, I'll tell you later," he said. "Here's the important part. You need to get over there now and find it. Otherwise someone else is going to beat us to the punch."

"We already went through that place," Emmanuelle said.

"I know, but somehow we missed it."

A pause.

"Meet me there," Emmanuelle said.

"I can't," Kong said. "I'm stuck in Macau and I'm supposed to have supper with someone. If I bolt out of here, it's going to look suspicious. Then I have something else going on tonight that's going to keep me tied up until after dark. I'll call you as soon as I'm free. But you need to get over there right now. In two or three hours it will probably be too late."

Okay.

She'd go now.

"Be careful," Kong said. "If someone else shows up, get the hell out of there. They're not the kind to play nice."

"Okay."

"I mean it."

"Okay."

"Don't screw with them."

"I said okay. So where should I look? Do you have any idea?"

"I don't know," Kong said. "All I know is that Pak has it, he definitely has it. He might have stashed it off-site, in a locker or something. Look for strange keys."

"Okay."

"I'll try to break free in an hour or two and give you more details on what's going on," he said. "Right now I have to run."

"Be careful."

"You too. By the way," Kong said. "If you find it, don't screw me over."

"I won't."

"Don't find it and then pretend you didn't find it," Kong said. "If you do, I'll know."

"I'm not going to screw you over," Emmanuelle

said. "If we find it, you more than earned your share."

93

August 10
Monday Afternoon

As soon as Prarie stepped into the alley, a man grabbed her and held a knife to her ribs. "Just give me a reason," he said in French. She stared into his eyes to gauge how serious he was. Those were the same eyes she saw just seconds ago in the printout of the man who had been asking about them. How did he know she would be coming out this way? Did he pay the elderly lady off? Was it a trap?

"Just do as you're told," he said. "I'm here to protect you."

"Bullshit!"

"Just give me two minutes and you'll understand."

He led her to a car and made her get in the passenger seat.

"Don't even think about shouting. I'm sorry to be so rough," he said. "I need you to listen while I tell you what's going on. The woman you're with—

Emmanuelle Laurent—killed your father. You're next unless you come to your senses."

"Bullshit."

"Let me show you something," the man said. He pulled a picture out of his wallet and stuck it in Prarie's face. It showed him and Emmanuelle with their arms around each other, smiling. "She used to be my lover," he said.

Prarie flashed back to moments ago, in the lobby when she asked Emmanuelle if she knew the face in the printout.

Emmanuelle said, "No."

That was a lie.

Emmanuelle had just lied to her, not more than two minutes ago.

"What did she do, to get you to cooperate?" he asked.

Prarie didn't know whether she should actually talk to the man or not. Then, suddenly, something about him felt right. Here was actually here to help.

She could tell.

"She told me she was with an insurance company," she said.

The man grunted.

"That's so like her," he said. "She's a genius when she needs to be. Trust me, there is no insurance company. That's nothing more than a blatant lie. She's out to get five original paintings and stick them in her own pocket. Once you outlive your usefulness, she's going to do the same thing to you that she did to your father."

Prarie swallowed.

"She'll be coming out any minute."

The man cranked over the engine.

"Too bad for her, we'll already be gone."

He pulled into thick Hong Kong traffic and said, "I can't believe you're still alive."

"Me too, actually."

"You've had close calls?"

Prarie nodded.

The man shook his head in disapproval. "Emmanuelle would put your life on the line a hundred times if she thought it would be to her advantage." A pause, then, "Trust, me, I know from firsthand experience."

Prarie studied his face.

It was a good face.

"What's your name?"

"Sebastian," he said. "Sebastian Dexteau. I'm from Paris."

"I already figured that much. Me too."

He smiled.

"Yes, I know," he said. "You can't believe what I've gone through to find you. And I can't believe I actually did. My suggestion is that we go straight to the airport and put you on a plane right away."

"Good idea."

They drove that way.

"What are you going to do, after I leave?" she asked.

He grunted.

"I don't even want to tell you," he said. "You'll think I'm nuts."

She cocked her head, curious.

"Tell me," she said.

"Okay," he said, "but no laughing out loud. You can do it quietly, to yourself, but don't do it out loud. You need to promise."

She promised.

"What I'm going to do is try to save her," Sebastian said, "before she gets in so deep that she can't get out."

Prarie studied him.

"You still love her," she said.

"Regretfully, yes."

Silence.

Then Prarie said, "You're going to need help."

He looked at her skeptically.

"You want to stick around to kill her, for killing your father," he said. "She's crazy and she deserves it, but I can't let you do that."

Prarie exhaled.

He was partly right.

"I need her to look me in the eyes and apologize," Prarie said. "That won't bring him back, I understand that, but maybe it will bring me some closure."

Sebastian looked skeptical.

"It won't," he said.

94

August 10
Monday Night

onday night it stormed. A monsoon rain poured out of a black Hong Kong sky. Fan Rae gave Teffinger a kiss shortly after dark, handed him some rope, reminded him she was going to be his sex slave when she got back in a couple of hours, and then left. Teffinger followed her in the Honda quite a ways to a place called Aberdeen Harbour. There, Fan Rae parked her car and headed towards the water on foot.

Teffinger followed, silently with a heavy heart, knowing that life as he knew it was minutes away from ending.

The rain was hard.

But it was also warm.

He didn't care about it.

Fan Rae took a position in the shadows and stared across the water. Teffinger wasn't sure what she was fixated on. The boat at the end of the dock, directly across the water, appeared to be an old decommissioned steel vessel that had been converted into living quarters.

Lights were on inside.

The rest of the boats on the dock were dark and abandoned.

He should have brought binoculars and cursed himself for not having the foresight. Someone was on board the steel vessel. Every so often, a dark silhouette passed behind one of the window coverings.

Teffinger's heart pounded.

D'Asia?

Was the silhouette d'Asia?

A dog laid on the deck, quiet but not asleep; unfettered by the storm and maybe even liking it after the heat of the day.

Suddenly a door opened and a woman stepped out, holding a bowl in her hands. The rain was coming down too hard to get a good look at her, but she had the same posture and size as d'Asia. She set the bowl in front of the dog, patted him on the head and went back to the door. Just before it closed, the light caught her just right.

D'Asia!

It was definitely d'Asia!

"I'll be damned."

Then something unexpected happened.

The black silhouette of a man appeared on the roof of the boat. He jumped down on cat feet, directly next to the dog, and stabbed a knife in the back of the animal's head before that head even raised halfway up. The canine flattened without making a sound.

Then the man crept towards the door.

The door that d'Asia had just gone in.

He opened it, stepped inside and shut it behind him.

Teffinger ran as fast as his legs let him to the end of the dock and dived into the water. As soon as he got to the surface he broke into his most powerful overhand stroke.

Seconds later, he muscled his heavy soaking body onto the dock, bounded onto the boat and busted through the door.

D'Asia was on her back.

Her face was bloody.

Her eyes were terrified.

A man was on top of her, straddling her chest.

He had a knife to her face, taunting her before he killed her.

Teffinger took two steps towards him and hurled his body through the air.

The man recoiled lightning fast.

Teffinger felt the knife sink into his chest.

He twisted.

The knife came with him.

As he pulled it out, the man ran towards the door.

Teffinger got a better look at him.

He was big, almost as big as Teffinger and strong as a python.

Teffinger's instinct was to let him go

His other instinct was to kill him.

The man was on the deck by the time Teffinger got to him.

He hurled his body through the air and caught the man on the back.

They tumbled over the side and fell into the water.

The entire world went black.

Teffinger heard nothing.

He saw nothing.

Then the man had his head in a stranglehold.

He pushed him even farther underwater.

Teffinger fought and twisted and pulled frantically at the man's arms. It did no good.

Air.

Air.

He needed air!

95

August 10
Monday Night

Teffinger went into something like a crocodile death roll and broke free. Then rage took over. He held the man underwater with every ounce of strength he had. After a long time, the man stopped moving. Teffinger didn't care. He kept him there, under the surface, for second after second, making absolutely positive he was dead.

Then he let go.

To his surprise, he was quite a ways from the boat.

He swam towards it, on his back, keeping his head above water where the air was.

Air.

Air.

So sweet.

He barely had enough strength to drag his beaten body out of the water and onto the dock.

Then something weird happened.

He heard noises, desperate noises, coming from

inside the boat.

He went in and what he saw he could hardly believe. Fan Rae and d'Asia were locked together on the floor, bloody, trying to kill each other with their bare hands.

D'Asia saw him and shouted, "Nick! Help me!"

Fan Rae turned her head, saw him and shouted, "Teffinger, help me!"

He stood there frozen.

Then he made a split-second decision and punched Fan Rae in the face.

She made a terrible gurgling sound, tried to get to her feet, and then collapsed.

Teffinger pulled d'Asia to her feet.

She hugged him tighter than he had ever been hugged before.

Her body felt so absolutely perfect against him.

Then she cried.

Teffinger stared at Fan Rae. She laid there not moving with her eyes closed, either unconscious or dead.

96

August 10
Monday Night

Teffinger bent down to see if Fan Rae was breathing. As he kneeled over her, an insane pain suddenly exploded on the back of his head and then everything went black.

He awoke some time later.

Everything was pitch-black.

He was sitting in water.

He couldn't move.

He realized he was tied and struggled against the ropes until his skin ripped.

It did no good.

There was no getting out.

He was dangerously close to engines.

They were running and pumping water into the boat.

He was in the engine compartment and the boat was sinking.

"Nick, are you conscious?"

The words startled him.

He thought he was alone.

"Fan Rae?"

"Yes," she said. "D'Asia did this. She's killing us."

Teffinger shouted.

Help!

Help!

His voice bounced off the walls and got sucked into the engines. No one would be able to hear him. He was in the bowls of the boat, with the compartment door shut, surrounded by a steel hull.

"I've already been shouting for ten minutes," Fan Rae said. "It's no use. I'm sorry I got you into this. I really am. This is my fault. I need to tell you something, while we still have time."

"Tell me what?"

Her words were jumbled and her brain wasn't moving in a straight line, but she answered questions when Teffinger asked them and, by the time she was finished, he understood what she wanted to tell him.

D'Asia was a hit woman.

She murdered people for a living.

All of her assignments came through a woman named Kam Lee, who owned a dungeon. Kam Lee wasn't the one who hired her, though. She was just the conduit. Someone else was the boss. But he or she would never disclose themselves, for security purposes.

D'Asia wanted to know who the boss was, so she'd have some leverage if she ever outlived her usefulness. She hired a private investigator by the name of Tanna Fan to find out who he was.

"Tanna Fan?"

"Right, she's my sister," Fan Rae said.

Tanna started the investigation by going after Kam Lee, who was the most direct link to the boss. She broke into Kam Lee's house. She broke into Kam Lee's dungeon. She took los of Kam Lee's papers and got lots on information but didn't come up with the link. Unfortunately, in the process, she got captured on a security tape. Kam Lee didn't know who was breaking into her stuff, or why, but told the boss about it.

"He then, in turn, hired d'Asia, through Kam Lee, to find the woman and bring her to the dungeon for an interrogation, after which she would be killed."

D'Asia had developed a fondness for Tanna by this point, so they had a discussion and made a deal.

D'Asia would capture Tanna and bring her to the dungeon. Tanna would be interrogated but wouldn't say who she was working for or why. Afterwards, d'Asia would take Tanna somewhere to kill her.

"The deal was, though, that d'Asia wouldn't really kill her," Fan Rae said. "She would really let her go and then report back that the job had been done and that the body had been disposed of."

They then executed that plan to perfection.

Obviously, Tanna couldn't be in Hong Kong any longer so she changed her name and moved to Rome. She didn't tell anyone that she was still alive, except for Fan Rae. That was absolutely necessary because if the boss ever found out that d'Asia deceived him, she would be killed herself.

So Tanna disappeared.

Her body never showed up.

Everyone thought she was dead.

End of story.

Except that the story didn't exactly end there.

"I knew that d'Asia was a hit woman because she had confided in Tanna who in turn confided in me," Fan Rae said. "I also owed d'Asia a favor, for letting Tanna live. It turned out that I drew one of the murders that d'Asia subsequently committed. I misdirected the investigation so she wouldn't be discovered. That's something I'm not proud of."

Time went on.

Nothing happened.

Everything was status quo.

The problem was that Tanna had a P.I partner by the name of Lily Yip, who actually thought Tanna had been murdered when she disappeared. Lily Yip got obsessed with finding Tanna's killer. She theorized that it was the hit woman who Tanna had for a client. Lily's theory was that the hit woman killed Tanna because Tanna knew her identity and posed a threat. Lily set out to find this hit woman.

Somehow she got some information that the woman had been assigned to hit a man in Denver, a man by the name of Nick Teffinger.

"That's right," Fan Rae said. "D'Asia didn't go there to get your help. She went there to murder you."

Lily Yip followed her to Denver.

She hung outside Teffinger's house.

She waited for d'Asia to show up.

She went in, in the middle of the night, and tried to kill her. "That's when you interceded," Fan Rae said. "D'Asia got the upper hand and managed to kill her."

"So the person who got killed in my bedroom is Lily Yip?"

"Correct."

It was.

"I don't know exactly why d'Asia didn't finish the job when she was in Denver," Fan Rae said. "As best as I can figure, she was going to kill you in your sleep. Then the attack happened. Then you wanted to call the local police department to report it. D'Asia didn't want her name and fingerprints and photograph in a police report so she left and came back to Hong Kong to bide her time."

Then Teffinger came to Hong Kong and told the whole story to Fan Rae.

"I recognized Lily Yip from the photos of her," Fan Rae said. "But I couldn't tell you anything because she was a direct link to Tanna, and if you started uncovering everything it would come to light that Tanna was still alive. So I had to deflect you from moment one."

"So you also knew who d'Asia was the whole time?"

"I did," Fan Rae said. "But I also knew she was a

killer and tried to steer you away from her."

Then something bad happened.

When Fan Rae told Tanna that Lily Yip had been killed by d'Asia in Denver, Tanna went nuts. She never liked d'Asia in the first place, since she was a hit woman. But when Lily got killed, that was it.

"Tanna came to Hong Kong to kill d'Asia," Fan Rae said. "I tried to talk her out of it but she was hell bent. She was going to do it tonight. She hooked up with some stranger named Kong who was going to help her. I came here tonight to keep Tanna safe from Kong, not to help her kill d'Asia."

The boat was dangerously low in the water.

"Some of the windows will go under pretty soon," Teffinger said. "When that happens, it'll just be a mater of minutes."

Silence.

"I love you," Fan Rae said. "I want you to know that before we die."

"Me too," he said. "I love you too. So know that, back."

Suddenly a voice came from behind them.

"Well, isn't this cute."

The words came from d'Asia.

"That's right," she said. "I've been sitting back there the whole time and I have to tell you, Teffinger, that Fan Rae got it all figured out correctly. I'm thoroughly impressed."

"D'Asia?"

"Shut up," she said. "Did you think I'd be dumb enough to just put you in a sinking boat and leave? Someone might notice it and come by to save you. So I just decided to let you sweat it out for a while. But Teffinger, you're right, the water's going to start coming in the windows pretty soon, meaning it's time for me to leave."

She turned a flashlight on and pointed it into Teffinger's eyes.

He must have squinted because she said, "Bright, isn't it?"

She walked over.

A long knife was in her right hand.

"Before I leave, I want to make absolutely sure that you're both dead," she said. "I'm sure you understand my position. So here's your choice. I'll either slit your throat or stab you in the back of the skull. You have five seconds to decide."

Teffinger pulled at the ropes with all his might.

They didn't budge, not an inch, not half an inch.

97

August 10
Monday Night

Prarie and Sebastian ended up at a house he was renting at the east end of the island, a short distance from where the Island Eastern Corridor ended. Sebastian had a computer and encouraged Prarie to log onto the net. She searched for the insurance company that Emmanuelle said she was working for. There was no such insurance company. Sebastian put an arm around her shoulders and gave her a comfort hug.

"I'm sorry you got dragged into this mess."

"It's not your fault."

"Yeah, I know, but still—"

Prarie's phone rang repeatedly all evening.

It was Emmanuelle calling.

Prarie didn't answer, not once.

They were letting the woman cool her heels.

Then, after dark, Sebastian used Prarie's phone to call Emmanuelle. "Surprise, he said, it's me. Prarie's with me. She's safe. She knows about your whole fake insurance company scam. She knows you're just trying to get the paintings for yourself. She knows you killed her father. Get a pencil, because I'm going to tell you where we're at."

He gave her directions.

"Come over, right now," he said. "We need to chat. It's time to stop all this insanity before it gets even worse."

He hung up and put his arm around Prarie. "You need to go somewhere safe before she get's here," he said. "You've outlived your usefulness to her at this point. Does she have a gun?"

No, she didn't.

"We had one and she wanted to keep it, but I threw it away," Prarie said.

"Smart move."

"Into the harbour," she added.

"Good place."

He cocked his head in thought.

"You should probably wait somewhere down the street," he said. "Take your cell phone with you. Don't come back until and unless I call and say the coast is clear. Does that sound like a good plan?"

It did.

"I need to use the facilities first," she said.

She used them, then left.

98

August 10
Monday Night

Prarie woke up and realized she had been unconscious. She was on a bed. Her arms were stretched tight above her head, with her hands near the headboard. When she went to sit up, she realized she was tied. Next to her was another woman, stretched out and tied in the same position—Emmanuelle.

"Are you conscious?" Emmanuelle said.

Her voice was quiet, barely a whisper.

"Yes."

"Talk quietly," Emmanuelle said. "We need to come up with a plan."

"You killed my father," Prarie said.

"No I didn't, he did," Emmanuelle said.

"Sebastian?"

"His name's not Sebastian," she said. "It's Jacques Girard."

"I don't understand what's going on."

"Understand this," Emmanuelle said. "He's going to find out everything we know about the paintings and then he's going to kill us."

"I don't get it."

"He took you in the alley to draw me in," Emmanuelle said. "I should have picked up some death stars before I came over."

Time passed, then more time.

"Where is he?" Prarie asked.

"He's making us sweat," Emmanuelle said. "That way we'll talk better. Let me tell you a few things."

Emmanuelle told Prarie that she had been romantically involved with Jacques Girard for two years. He was rich and nice when they met, but later got intense and irritable. He learned that Van Gogh's "Self Portrait" was for sale on the black market. He had two reputable people authenticate it and then bought it for an insane amount of money. He later learned that he actually bought a fake. The two men who authenticated it said that what he had now wasn't the same painting they were shown. He came to the conclusion that the original painting had been switched out at the last second by the broker, Vance Wu.

Vance Wu, in turn, had dropped off the face of the earth.

Girard then hired a P.I. by the name of Quinton Benabent to find Wu and figure out what was going on.

Girard wanted the painting back.

It wasn't just the money.

It was the fact that someone had played him for a fool.

Benabent was being paid well.

He dug deep and hard.

He came up with a theory that Prarie's father, Jean-Didier Dubois, had been involved in the initial theft of the paintings from Musee d'Orsay. Jean-Didier had since left the museum to become a cab driver. Benabent tried to get information out of Jean-Didier, who confessed that five paintings had been stolen, but wouldn't cooperate in giving up any information on the people involved—probably, because if he did, it would put Prarie in jeopardy.

Benabent was a smart man.

But he wasn't violent.

When Jean-Didier wouldn't talk, that's when Jacques Girard lost it.

He went to interrogate Jean-Didier himself.

When the man wouldn't cooperate, Girard shot him in the back of the head in his own taxi and made it look like a robbery.

"I knew everything that was going on," Emmanuelle said. "When he killed Jean-Didier, that was too much for me. I couldn't tell the police, first because he left no proof behind, but more importantly because I knew he'd kill me. I knew I had to get away from him and I did. By that point, though, I also knew that there were five original paintings out there in the world somewhere. I knew that Girard would go after you next. And I also knew that you could help me find the paintings. So I came up with a plan to pretend I was working with an insurance company and got you to help me. That was partly for me, but it was mostly for you. I wanted to get you out of Paris so Girard couldn't get his claws into you. I knew he'd kill you if you didn't cooperate."

Silence.

"Somehow he tracked us to our hotel," Emmanuelle said. "When the lady showed us the printout of his face, sure, I knew who he was, but what was I supposed to do? Stop and explain everything to you on the spot? I just wanted to get out of there. In hindsight, that lady must have tipped him off, and must have been paid to get us to head to the alley. When you came out alone, he figured that was good enough. All he needed to do was use you for bait to draw me in."

Prarie exhaled.

"This is all so twisted," she said.

"Yes it is."

"So you never intended to return the paintings at all?" Prarie asked. "You intended to keep them for yourself?"

"That part is true," Emmanuelle said. "But I was going to give half of whatever we recovered to you. You could return your half if you wanted." A pause, then, "By the way, there's one more thing you should probably know."

Really?

What?

"You remember that I formed that alliance with Kong, after he took me to the dungeon, and I agreed to cut him in if we recovered anything, right?"

Yes.

Of course she remembered.

"Well, he called me today," Emmanuelle said. "He had information that one of the original paintings ended up with the artist, Guotin Pak."

"How did he know that?"

"That's a long story," Emmanuelle said. "The short of it is that he told me to get over there, right that minute, and find it before some other people showed up. I never made it, though, because I've been looking for you all day. That painting is gone by now."

Ouch.

"Kong called me again, about an hour later when he got a chance to talk in more detail, and he told me the whole background of how the paintings got stolen from Musee d'Orsay, and sold, and fakes got switched, and stuff like that. He got the entire story from a man named Jack Poon, who is behind the whole scheme. Anyway, the gist of all that is that Vance Wu ended up with one of the originals. Poon had already deployed his men to recover it. The other three originals were sold around the world, to buyers in Cairo, Rome and Madrid. What that means to us is that all five paintings are now gone."

"So we did all this for nothing," Prarie said.

"In hindsight, yes."

"And now we get to die for it."

"Right."

Rustling noises came from the other room.
"Here he comes," Emmanuelle said.
Prarie pulled at the ropes.
They didn't budge.

99

August 10
Monday Afternoon

A figure stepped into the bedroom. Prarie turned her head. The figure wasn't a man. It was a young Chinese woman, about twenty. She looked like she'd been through the war. She stepped back out, then returned a few moments later with a knife and cut them loose.

She didn't speak English or French but told them her name.

It was Syling Wu.

She led them into the basement. It was obvious that she had been a prisoner there for some time. Jacques Girard was on the floor, dead with a fork in his eye and a serious wound to the back of his head.

Prarie and Emmanuelle hugged the woman.

"I don't know who you are or how you got the upper hand, but he had it coming," Emmanuelle said. "He had every bit of it coming."

They called the police, anonymously, but left before they showed up and headed to Guotin Pak's house on the bluff. The place was trashed. Someone had beaten them there and tore the place apart. The walls were gutted. The ceiling was pulled down. The floor was pulled up.

"We're too late," Emmanuelle said.

"Oh, well, we had to try."

"Right."

The only thing left intact was the painting in progress, still sitting there in the middle of the room, worthless.

They went outside and sat down on the steps.

"Now what?" Prarie asked.

Emmanuelle shrugged.

"Now we get the hell out of Hong Kong while we're still alive."

They got in the car.

Emmanuelle cranked up the engine but didn't take off. She just sat there behind the wheel.

"What are you waiting for?" Prarie asked.

Emmanuelle turned the engine off and got out.

"I want check something," she said.

Inside, behind the work in progress, they found a second painting, tacked on the stretcher bars, protected with a plastic barrier.

Claude Monet's "Poppies."

The original.

"I'll be damned," Prarie said. "He hid it in plain sight."

They carefully rolled it up and sealed it a cylindrical tube, set it in the backseat and drove into the storm, looking for a hotel. On the way, Emmanuelle said, "I've been thinking."

"Yeah?"

"Yeah. With what we found out ourselves, combined with what Kong told me, we pretty much know the whole story of what happened. The other four paintings are beyond our reach. What we can do though, at this point, is send an anonymous email to Musee d'Orsay, the Hong Kong police and the Paris police, setting out the whole story, including the names of the people who have the other four paintings. We'd need to be careful to not say anything that will implicate us in an illegal activity, but that's doable. Armed with that information, they should be able to recover the other four. Your father's legacy and reputation will be restored, to the extent it can. That's what you wanted, right?"

Right, it was.

"Except I was hoping to get all five back," Prarie said.

Emmanuelle chuckled.

"That isn't going to happen, girlfriend," she said. "I've gone through too much brain damage to give up number five. It's mine—ours, actually, half is yours. Plus Kong gets his cut."

"I don't want my half," Prarie said.

"Okay, then, it's mine," Emmanuelle said. "I deserve something for all this, don't you think?"

Prarie considered it.

The answer surprised her.

"Yes. You do."

100

August 10
Monday Night

D'Asia pressed the knife against Teffinger's throat. "I'm actually sort of sorry to see it end this way," she said. "You did, after all, travel halfway around the world to help me. Then you get killed for all your troubles. It doesn't seem fair, does it?" Silence. "It's nothing personal, Teffinger. It's just a contract, and a contract is a contract. When I get them, I fill them. It's called maintaining my reputation. Do you have any last words? Do you want to say goodbye to Fan Rae one more time?"

"No," Teffinger said.

"No?"

"No."

"Okay then."

"I do have one thing to say to you, though," he said.

She pushed the knife harder against his throat.

"Go ahead, but I'll warn you in advance not to

piss me off."

He exhaled.

"Can you scratch my nose?" he asked.

She chuckled.

"If you're planning on some lamebrain sudden move, it's not going to work," she said. "Save your strength."

"Actually, it really does itch," he said.

She looked at him, then scratched his nose.

He made no moves.

"Thanks," he said. "That's a lot better. Before you kill me, I want you to think about something. You're killing me because you have a contract to do it. Has it occurred to you yet that the person who gave you that contract has fired you?"

Silence.

"What do you mean?"

"What I mean is this," he said. "The guy who just attacked you upstairs, the one I saved you from, where do you think he came from?"

She chuckled.

"He's a friend of Tanna's," she said.

"Yes and no," Teffinger said. "Tanna's picture was in the newspaper Sunday morning, in the entertainment section. Did you know that?"

"No, and I don't really care."

"Me and Fan Rae were partying with Yuki, the singer, at the Dragon-i," he said. "Tanna was there too. So were the paparazzi. The next day, there were pictures in the newspaper. Tanna was in those pictures. She was sitting on a couch, in the background, but there was no mistaking it was her."

"So what?"

"So here's what I think happened," Teffinger said. "The man who gave you the initial contract to kill her saw her in the paper. He then realized you lied, when you said you killed her and disposed of the body. He then put a contract out on you because you lied to him and couldn't be trusted any longer. The guy upstairs was the hitman for that contract."

D'Asia chewed on it.

"You have no job left," Teffinger said. "When you show back up, and say that you killed me, they'll just take that opportunity to wipe you off the face of the earth. Wham, you're gone. Nighty-night, little angel."

She stared at him.

Her face started to change.

"Here's what we can do," Teffinger said. "You let me and Fan Rae go and we'll let you go. We all go our separate ways. You can disappear. You're a marked woman and need to get out of Hong Kong in any event. You have the money saved up to do it."

D'Asia stood up and paced.

Then she said, "What about Tanna? She's still out to kill me."

"When we tell her you let us go, she'll back off," Teffinger said. "An eye for an eye."

D'Asia pointed the flashlight at Fan Rae.

"That's true," Fan Rae said. "I'll personally guarantee that she backs off. Everything will be even. No more killing, no more looking over our shoulders, either direction."

D'Asia continued pacing.

Then she cut the ropes on Teffinger's hands, handed him the knife and flashlight, and ran out the door.

ABOUT THE AUTHOR

Formerly a longstanding trial attorney before taking the big leap and devoting his fulltime attention to writing, R.J. Jagger (that's a penname, by the way) is the author of over twenty hard-edged mystery and suspense thrillers. In addition to his own books, Jagger also ghostwrites for a well-known, bestselling author. He is a member of the International Thriller Writers and the Mystery Writers of America. His books are all complete within their own four corners and can be read in any order.

RJJagger.com

www.ingramcontent.com/pod-product-compliance
Lightning Source LLC
Chambersburg PA
CBHW030702190726

48286CB00001B/134